Sam Hawkins Pirate Detective

and the Pointy Head Lighthouse

Ian Billings is a writer, teacher, actor and juggler. He is five feet seven inches tall standing in his socks, and the same length lying down. His hobbies include hiccupping, wobbling jelly and hiding behind curtains. He has written for BBC TV's *ChuckleVision* and his pantomimes and plays have been performed all over Britain from Swindon to Wolverhampton and back again. Ian's secret for successful writing is getting the page numbers in the right order and not falling off his chair. He would like to thank the English alphabet for its contribution to this book.

Here's a swashbuckling selection of some of the wave reviews Ian received for his first book, SAM HAWKINS PIRATE DETECTIVE AND THE CASE OF THE CUT-GLASS CUTLASS:

'Of all the detectives in the world Sam Hawkins is one of them' – *Daily Splash*

'A harrowing, down to earth tale of human endurance against almost invincible opposition' – *Grog-making Monthly* (about a different book)

'Sam Hawkins was fired with enthusiasm' – reference from Sam's last job

'Not enough cheese' – *Cheese-lovers' Weekly*

Also by Ian Billings

Sam Hawkins Pirate Detective
and the Case of the Cut-glass Cutlass

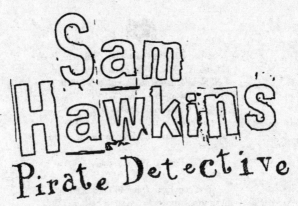

Sam Hawkins

Pirate Detective

and the Pointy Head Lighthouse

IAN BILLING

Illustrated by Sarah Nayler

MACMILLAN CHILDREN'S BOOKS

First published 2004 by Macmillan Children's Books
a division of Macmillan Publishers Limited
20 New Wharf Road, London N1 9RR
Basingstoke and Oxford
www.panmacmillan.com

Associated companies throughout the world

ISBN 0 330 41498 4

Text copyright © Ian Billings 2004
Illustrations copyright © Sarah Nayler 2004

1 3 5 7 9 8 6 4 2

A CIP catalogue record for this book is available from
the British Library.

Printed and bound in Great Britain by Mackays of Chatham plc, Kent

For Stephanie Dale, of course!

Chapter One

Call me Hawkins, Sam Hawkins! The greatest buccaneer to sail the seven seas! Sam Hawkins, the swishiest swashbuckler in the land! Sam Hawkins, the finest pirate ever to put his shoulder to the tiller.

One year ago my face was the talk of the town, fêted and photographed from Pointy Head to Clapshot Towers. One year ago I was Sam Hawkins, the man who discovered the stolen Cut-glass Cutlass. One year ago I was loved by the public. But fame comes and fame goes, and mine went. Nobody recognizes me any more – though small children do point at me in the street.

I was standing beside my hammock in my bedroom, dressed in a newly bought tracksuit with my head bedecked in a sweatband. On my shoulder was my constant companion, Spot the Parrot. He seemed to be tutting quietly.

'I need to keep trim, Spot. I'm getting a little tubby about the hull and 'tis time to get fit!'

And so I began.

'Stretch . . . 2 . . . 3 . . . 4!'

So what if I was a one-ship wonder? So what if my success was just a flash in the pan? My history is a noble one and I can weather such fleeting storms.

'Touch toes . . . 2 . . . 3 . . . 4!'

Though I was born in England, my family had previously lived long and hard upon the Caribbean island of Jataka. Sadly, they were deported in slightly embarrassing circumstances shortly before my arrival. My mother, 'Grapeshot' Betty Hawkins, berthed me and the rest of the family in the town of Washed-upon-the-Beach.

'And star-jumps . . . 2 . . . 3 . . . 4!'

I soon took up the family trade – piracy. With my ship, *Scuttle Butt*, I plundered and pillaged every port from Land's End to Santa Cruz. I've smuggled halibut with 'One Elbow' Charlotte, who could whistle a sea shanty through her ear, I've kidnapped sea-horses owned by Sheikh El Fah Letha, I've poked crabs through the letter box of Lady Tottering and I've even been taught to yodel by an Eskimo. But that was long, long ago, and in time I threw in the anchor on my piratical ways and took up a more useful pursuit. I became the world's first pirate detective.

'Stretch to the side . . . 2 . . . 3 . . . 4!'

'Twas a merry maiden voyage, and cracking my first case will go down in local history. But 'twould be an immodest buccaneer to claim all the crime-busting credit for himself. Where would I be without my crew, Lan Ho and Molly Meakins? I pondered the question for a moment. Where indeed? Truth be told, they are the finest crew members with whom I have ever sailed.

I rescued Lan Ho, my wily and wise Chinese cook and cabin boy, from certain death in the choppy waters of Kowloon Bay, Hong Kong. He's forever grateful for my gesture. He mentions it most days. We've sliced and spliced our ways through many piratical adventures and no escapade would be complete without him.

Molly Meakins, the finest woman ever to weigh anchor, could tie a bowline with one hand and gut a haddock with the other. I'd netted her from a Norwegian trawler many years back and she's been loyal to me ever since. She can reduce a man to tears with just her feet – she should wash them more often.

And, of course, Spot the Parrot, who has sat on my shoulder through thick and thin – mostly thick – for many a year.

'Jumping on the spot . . . 2 . . . 3 . . . 4!'

The parrot squawked indignantly and flew from

the room.

'Sorry, Spot! Press-ups . . . 2 . . . 3 . . . 4!'

Nobody seems to want me any more. The crime rate in Washed-upon-the-Beach was at low tide and no naughty-deed-doers were doing any naughty deeds. Flotsam and jetsam! And we were running out of cash. The Naughty Lass takes a lot of paying for. It may be a council house to most folk, but, dressed up, it could easily pass for a seaworthy vessel – well, almost.

I, Sam Hawkins, had finally reached a decision. 'Twas not one I had taken lightly. Oh, no. I had tossed and turned in my hammock for many a night. But the time had come to bite the mullet and face the crew. 'Twas time to throw in the anchor and give up being detectives. There was no two ways about it. We hadn't had a nibble of a case in months.

As I peeled off my tracksuit and eeled into my clothes, I wondered what other careers my crew could pursue. I could make a few pennies playing my squeeze-box, I suppose. Molly could be a nightclub bouncer – she's built like a portly tug.

I looked at *Keeping Fit for Sailors: A Book of Naval Manoeuvres*. I had already read the first two chapters. With a bit of luck I'd have it all finished by next week-end. And then, with a bit more luck, I could start doing the exercises! Suddenly, I heard a loud explosion from downstairs.

4

'Ah!' I said, tying my neckerchief. 'Breakfast!'

In the kitchen Ho was using a ladle to bang a saucepan that was giving off a pong worse than a ton of rotting seaweed.

'Whatever is that?' I demanded, holding my nose as I hove into the room.

'Toast!' he yelled, running the saucepan under the tap.

'But you don't make toast in a saucepan, you wet fish, you make toast in the toaster.'

I picked up the toaster and waggled it in front of his confused face.

'Don't touch that, boss!'

'Why not?'

'Because the eggs are nearly done!'

'But you don't cook eggs in a toaster, you – Oh, never mind.'

At which point Molly thundered into the room.

'Someone's sat on my quiver!' she bellowed.

She then flung a chair out of the way and clomped over to Ho. In her banana-bunched hand she clutched her precious quiver.

Molly, one of the finest archers at sea, Bull's-eye Molly, as she was once known, could hit a target at 100 metres. But not with bent arrows. And being a seagull-eyed detective, I immediately noticed a dint in her quiver.

'Whoever's bottom fits this dint is the person who bent my arrows!'

She placed the bent quiver against Ho's bottom, but his was far too small a bottom to make such a dint. She tried it against my ample stern. No, 'twas not mine either. That book of exercises was a wise investment.

She banged the quiver on the breakfast table.

'Then who could have sat on my quiver?'

Ho and I quietly took the quiver from the table and measured it against Molly's bottom. A perfect fit.

'Oh, cuttlefish!' she swore, and sat down.

'Cuttlefish, cuttlefish!' echoed Spot the Parrot.

Ho slid two steaming plates before us and stood back with a pleased look on his face. Molly poked the breakfast with an arrow.

'What's that?'

'Toast on egg!' said Ho proudly.

'I don't like toast on egg!' said Molly.

'It's porridge, then,' said Ho.

'I like porridge!' said Molly, and set to work slurping her way through it.

I bravely joined in, but it tasted like a heron's knee. I decided the time had come to make an announcement. I leapt to my feet and banged the salty cellar on the table to gain my crew's attention.

'Crew members of the Naughty Lass, lend me your ears! We need to discuss our future. We need to discuss how we are to plough through the waters of our financial misfortune. We need—'

'Twas at that point a knock came to the door. A knock and a ring.

Strange, I thought, why would someone be ringing *and* knocking?

'Ho,' I ordered, 'answer the door!'

Ho looked at me in that *way* he has.

'Molly, answer the door!'

'I'm slurping!' she said, mid-slurp.

'Very well, *I* shall answer the door. You two, stay here and carry on with what you are doing!'

I toddled down the corridor, wiping remnants of breakfast from my chin, and threw open the front door.

'Heave-ho!' I announced. 'Welcome aboard the Naughty Lass, home of award-winning Pirate Detective, Sam Hawkins!'

Before me stood a little man. If he'd been a vegetable he'd have been a sprout, if you see what I mean. He wore a thick fisherman's jumper and blue dungarees.

'We are Billy Buddy!' he announced. 'Can we come in?'

I looked about for a second person, but there was

only this solitary sole on my doormat.

'Certainly,' I said nervously.

He stepped into the hallway and I led him to the lounge.

'Please take a seat!' I said, gesturing towards my most comfy settee.

At that point something strange happened. My visitor's voice changed.

'*No, thanks. We'd prefer to stand!*'

'Twas a gruff and grumpy voice, completely unlike the jolly tones I'd heard earlier. And as suddenly as it had changed, it switched back again.

'No, I think we'd like to sit!' 'Twas the first voice again.

I'd heard of many strange happenings from my days on the bubbling briny, but never a man with two voices.

'*Stand!*' said the second voice insistently.

'Sit!' said the first.

Suddenly the man grabbed his left hand and held it up behind his back. Bemused by this bizarre sight, I slowly retreated towards the fireplace.

'*I want to stand!*'

He forced the hand back to the front of his body and the two hands pushed against each other. They were both trying to gain, well, the upper hand.

This went on for a few moments. Billy Buddy

looked as if he was wrestling with the lid of an invisible jar.

'Perhaps I could offer you . . . er . . . both . . . some tea?' I suggested, trying to take control of the situation.

'Lovely!' said the first voice, and the man sat down.

'*I only drink coffee,*' said the second, and he stood up.

'Right, that's it!' said the first voice. The man suddenly grabbed himself by the scruff of the neck and walked himself to the door. 'Outside, now!' And with that he hurled himself into the corridor and slammed the door.

I scurried over and heard muffled oaths and the occasional slap. The slap became a thump, then all fell silent.

The door slowly swung open and the man returned.

'Now say sorry!'

'*Sorry!*'

He collapsed on the settee and stared at me. I was lost for words. I fingered the ship's bell and wondered whether to summon my crew for assistance. I dinged it gently and Molly and Ho appeared.

The man jumped to his feet and shook hands with Molly.

'How do you do? *How do you do?*' he said, in both

his voices.

Molly shook his hand suspiciously and sat down.

He grabbed Ho's hand.

'How do you do? *How do you do?*'

Ho sat behind Molly for protection. They both looked to me.

'Now,' I said, 'how can we be of service?'

The man stretched back on the settee and began to talk.

'We need help. We are Billy Buddy, keeper of the Pointy Head Lighthouse, and something most strange and mysterious has happened.'

'Go on,' I said, sniffing a mystery.

''Twas a dark and stormy night—'

'*Actually, it was more like a moonlit night.*'

'Cold and bitter.'

'*Quite mild, I thought.*'

'Who's telling this story, you or me?'

This was a question we were all asking. I decided to seize the moment and take charge.

'Hold fast!' I announced. 'Why doesn't one of you tell the tale?'

'Very well,' he said. Then looked at me.

'*Which one?*'

I was stumped for an answer. Quick-witted Ho came to the rescue and pointed at the man.

'You!' he said.

'Very well. 'Twas a dark and stormy night last night. The cliffs of Washed-upon-the-Beach were lashed and splashed with the cold spray of the tempestuous storm. We, Billy Buddy, were cleaning old Bessie, our light bulb, so she could shine brightly and proudly across the ocean and warn sailors of the dangers that lay about. So there we were, atop our long ladder, a duster in our hands. We heard a crack. 'Twas a crack to deafen a whale. A crack followed by a shudder. At that point the whole of the Pointy Head Lighthouse started to shake and sway. We gathered our thoughts and our dusters, slid down the ladder and scrambled from the light-house into the darkness. As the rain pelted our face, we paused by a bush. But we could see nothing in the storm – the lighthouse was shrouded in a veil of dark drizzle—'

'*Oh, very well put!*'

'Thank you . . . and we heard a roar and a crunch like no other at sea. Something horrid was happening to our precious lighthouse. And the sound was like the howl of a sea monster—'

'*It didn't sound like a sea monster to me . . .*'

He placed a finger on his lip, silencing his second voice, then continued.

'And so, fearing for our lives, we scuttled away from the Pointy Head Lighthouse that had been our home

for nearly thirty years and hid and shivered in a nearby cave. And there we waited out the storm.'

I pulled a quill from my tunic and began making notes.

''Tis a strange tale,' I said.

'And gets stranger still. When we awoke this morning, we returned to the lighthouse and . . . and . . .'

He began to sniff in his second voice.

'Pull yourself together!' he shouted.

'*Sorry!*' he mumbled.

'And . . . the lighthouse was gone! Vanished!'

Ho was looking at Billy Buddy inquisitively.

'How can a lighthouse vanish?' he asked.

'That's what we've come to ask you. Please find our lighthouse, Mr Hawkins.'

'Well, 'tis certainly an intriguing case. But old Slice-'em and Dice-'em Hawkins has never baulked at a challenge.' I stood proudly and plunged my finger into the air. 'Sam Hawkins will take on your case!'

Billy Buddy leapt to his feet and began shaking all our hands.

'Thank you! *Thank you!* Thank you! *Thank you!* Thank you! *Thank you!*'

He started to make his way to the front door. I followed behind.

'Thank you, Mr Hawkins, you will make a couple of old men very happy!'

'You're welcome! Now, the matter of my fee—'

'Should you need us, we'll be staying at the Red Sea Lion Tavern.'

He turned and, with a jaunty double-handed salute, was gone.

As I returned to the lounge I heard a tidal wave of giggles.

Molly and Ho were holding their sides on the settee.

'So what's the cause of all this jollity?' I asked, miffed that they were cracking jokes without me.

'But don't you see, boss, it's *so* obvious,' giggled Ho.

I toyed with my quill.

'I . . . I know it's obvious. Obviously it's obvious.' I sat down. 'Which is the obvious bit?'

'Billy Buddy has spent so much time alone at the Pointy Head Lighthouse, he's started talking to himself.'

Molly joined in. 'Billy Buddy's been talking to himself for so long, he thinks he's two different people.'

They collapsed into a heap of chuckles.

'So what's happened to the lighthouse?'

The laughter stopped.

'No idea.'

What can I tell you of the Pointy Head Lighthouse? Its beaming lamp has shone across the sea for many a year. 'Tis a legendary lighthouse, spoken of with awe by sailors and pirates alike. After years of travel across the watery waves, a glimpse of the Pointy Head Lighthouse was the first sign of home to many a buccaneer.

I was determined to solve this case. If the Pointy Head Lighthouse meant a lot to me, it might mean a lot to a lot more. If I discovered its whereabouts, I would become famous again – an A-list pirate detective once again.

I smiled at the thought.

However, a number of other thoughts swirled and whirled in my nautical brain:

I made some notes.

1) *Has the Pointy Head Lighthouse really been stolen?*
2) *Who would steal a lighthouse?*
3) *How do you steal a lighthouse?*
4) *Where would you put it?*

And, most of all:

5) *Why?*

14

Batten down the hatches! Box the compass! Lash the trinkets to the deck! Sam Hawkins, Pirate Detective, was setting sail on his greatest adventure ever! If only I could remember where I'd put my hat.

Chapter Two

Ha! This was a case to place Sam Hawkins back on the pirate private-eye map! Whether this voyage would be long and arduous or over in the twinkling of a duck's eye, I could not say, but from what my shell-like ear had heard so far, 'twould prove an interesting case.

Ho and Molly were left with instructions to finish the washing-up. If they were good, they could join me later. I dusted off my hat, stomped out of the Naughty Lass and climbed aboard the Nippy Clipper.

The Nippy Clipper was our motorbike and sidecar, which Ho kept spick and span. I kick-started the engine, which roared into life, and I was off. I sped along the streets of Washed-upon-the-Beach at a rare rate of knots, sniffing the sea breeze and feeling the wind in my hair. It felt good to be back on the trail of a case. Ha! Double ha!

Putt! Putt! Putt!

Ready to right wrongs . . .

Putt! Putt! Putt!

Bring naughty folk to justice . . .

Putt! Putt! Putt!

Whatever was that strange sound? 'Twas coming from between my knees. On closer inspection, 'twas coming from the engine. Curses! Ho was in charge of looking after the Nippy Clipper and 'twas clear he'd not looked after it well. 'Twas needing some feeding. Its little fuel gauge was telling me it wanted some of that petroleum stuff. I squinted my eagle eye across the surroundings. Nothing but fields and sheep. Oh, cockles! This was my first tasty case in months and I'd stumbled at the first ditch! Oh, mussels! I pulled the Nippy Clipper over by a nearby hedge.

I tried the key in its little starting hole. The engine gave off nothing but a putt-putt and the bad bike refused to move.

'If you were one of my crew, I'd have flogged you for this!' I sneered, but it made no difference.

Now it can't be far to the nearest petrol station, I thought. I umphed myself on to the saddle of the bike and gazed over the hedge. Fluttering in the distance was a sign I recognized. 'Twas a flapping flag that read 'Sea Shell' – a petrol station.

All I needed to do was push the Nippy Clipper over

there, fill her up and I'd be back on my merry way.

Now, what my naval noggin had failed to figure was the fact that the petrol station was not as close as its flag suggested. There it was, flapping and fluttering and luring me towards it. I thought it would be just over the hill, but no. 'Twas up a hill, down a dale, round a corner then two hairpin bends and over a cattlegrid.

I drew up at the station pooped as a puffin and leaned the bike against a pump.

'Twas at that point something odd happened. A voice spoke to me. A deep and thunderous voice from above.

'Congratulations!' it said.

I looked about me, but saw not a thing.

'Well done!' it said.

I looked all around. What was it?

'You are the thousandth visitor to Sea Shell petrol station! Choose a prize!'

At that point a small woman in oily overalls emerged from the shop part of the petrol station clutching a small micronophone and a clipboard. She scuttled towards me with a determined gait, a photographer following in her wake.

I realized at once who it was – Oil Flo! In days gone

by she used to grease the tiller of my old ship, *Scuttle Butt*. She'd done well for herself over the years.

We greeted each other like the old swabbies we were, but I was too breathless for conversation. The photographer flashed a few snaps for the local paper and disappeared.

'Now, Sam, here's your prize,' she said, waving the clipboard at me.

'Oh, just fill her up!' I said, panting.

'Okey-dokey!' she replied, and scurried off.

I wandered away while Flo filled up the bike.

At the edge of the station I looked once more over the fields and tried to work out a route towards the last-known sighting of the Pointy Head Lighthouse. Of course, I didn't need a map, because I knew Washed-upon-the-Beach like the back of my hand. I looked at the back of my hand and saw a spot I'd never seen before.

'Done!' bellowed Flo from the pump.

I turned, and a surprising sight met my eyes. The sidecar was full of toilet rolls.

'What's this?' I demanded.

'You told me to fill her up,' explained Flo, 'so I filled her up with your prize – 100 toilet rolls!'

Now, I wasn't going to look a gift sea-horse in the mouth, so I gracefully accepted the prize.

'Did you put petrol in too?'

'I certainly did, Sammy! Twenty pounds please!'

I parted with the money and was soon on my way – a jolly song in my heart, the wind in my hair and 100 free toilet rolls in my sidecar.

I pulled up at the Pointy Head Lighthouse and dismounted. When I say the Pointy Head Lighthouse, I don't, of course, mean the Pointy Head Lighthouse, I mean what was left of it – which was nothing more than a small pile of bricks and a doorstep.

Huddled by the remnants was old Billy Buddy. I hurried over to him and doffed my hat respectfully.

'I'm very sorry about your loss, Billy!' I said, placing a comforting hand on his shoulder.

'This was my home!' he said, as a pearl of a tear emerged from one eye.

'*Tatty old place, though!*' he said, in his second voice.

'That's because you never lifted a finger to do the dusting!'

'*How dare you!*'

I could feel another argument coming on, so I took swift action.

'Now, then, you two . . . this is no time for petty squabbling. We have a crime to solve. Understand?'

Billy Buddy nodded his head.

'Yes.'

'*Sorry!*'

I took him by the shoulder and we walked over to the cliffs. We stood in silence, looking out at the choppy water. In the distance a lone gull swooped.

'Now, Billy – and I want only one of you to answer this – have you any idea who might want this light-house?'

'No! No idea!'

'*What about Harvey Clump?*'

'Shhh!!!'

'*Shhh!*'

Billy Buddy shushed himself and refused to mention the name again. I made a mental note to find out more, but for now left him sniffing by the doorstep.

I investigated the remains of the lighthouse. 'Twas clear to my well-trained eye that the vile villains who'd snaffled the lighthouse had covered their tracks well. Not a single footprint was to be found on the ground, nor a giveaway fingerprint on the bricks. Nothing. 'Twas like the most deserted of desert islands.

'No clues here, then!' I cried, waving farewell to Billy Buddy and returning to the Nippy Clipper.

As I sped along the back roads of Washed-upon-the-Beach who should pass me, going in the opposite direction, but old Stump and Stibbins. I'd tangled with them before. They were the local police force. More like a police farce, I laughed, and swallowed a fly.

21

They eyed me suspiciously as I went by.

I hadn't gone much further along the road when a small boy dropped from the sky and landed in the sidecar. I've seen many strange things in my days at sea – a dolphin with two blowholes, for example, and old 'Gurgling' Tom's bendy-finger trick – but nothing had prepared me for this.

I skidded to a screeching halt, leaping from the bike in surprise. I was so stunned that I forgot to drop the foot. The bike keeled over on its side, unloading 100 toilet rolls and one small boy.

'What in the bluest of blue brinies is a-going on?' I barked.

I then quickly gathered my thoughts, plus a few toilet rolls, and stumbled over to the boy, who was lying on his back.

He was wearing a uniform, I noticed, but not a school uniform. 'Twas more like a military one. I saw a badge on his chest, it read 'Sea Scouts'.

'You're a Sea Scout!' I deftly deduced.

At those words, the Sea Scout mumbled something and his little eyes flickered.

I placed my shell-like ear to his lips and listened.

'Monkey . . .' he said softly.

I looked about. Had he lost his monkey? What was

all this drivel?

'What monkey?' I demanded.

He mumbled again. 'Monkey . . .' He took a breath. 'Bridge!'

I was confused.

'You can't play bridge with a monkey, though I do know a parrot who's very good at poker!'

He stirred and his eyes opened fully.

'No, no – I've just fallen off a monkey bridge!' He leaned up on his elbow. 'It was slung across the road and you were passing underneath. Good job you had all those toilet rolls in the sidecar!' He moaned a little. 'My arm!'

'Avast there, matey, fret not.' I swung my arm back and forth before him. 'Can you still do this?'

He tried.

'No, I can't!' he cried, worried.

'Don't worry,' I said comfortingly. 'Neither can I!'

'Take me back to where I came from!'

I looked up at the sky.

'Hmmmm . . .'

'No, no, my scout camp!'

'Where's that, then?'

'Just behind this hedge!'

I knew I was being a little blown off-course by this

occurrence, but a child was in need and a pirate detective has to go with the flow.

I helped the scout, whose name turned out to be Bobby, into the sidecar, threw the toilet rolls on top of him and drove into the nearby field.

The sight that met my windswept eyes was a marvellous one. The field was riddled with jolly Sea Scouts, all engaged in some task or other. They were building wooden ships, or pointing at the clouds, or cooking by a fire. 'Twas like watching a well-trained army of ants at work. Well, big ants, that is – ants in uniform . . . but you get the idea.

I pulled over by the largest tent, which, I assumed, belonged to their leader. I was right.

The tent flaps slapped open and out stepped a short, rotund man with odd teeth and a ginger moustache. He straightened his neckerchief and brushed his hair.

'I'm Able Seaman Christopher Wave! Welcome aboard!' I held out my hand and he suddenly shouted, 'Visitor on deck!'

With that cry, each and every Sea Scout in the field ceased his activity and produced a small kazoo from his pocket.

The tune they played was not one I recognized. I'm not sure it was one they recognized either. I was going to ask the able seaman about it, but he was too busy

24

standing to attention.

The tune finished and every Sea Scout saluted me. I waved back. And then they returned to their business.

'You haven't lost one, have you?' I asked, nodding towards the mass of scouty lads.

'Probably. Every time we come back from camp, there's one or two gone missing.'

I gestured towards the sidecar. Bobby was draped over the toilet rolls, gibbering to himself.

'Bobby Buoy! Not again.'

'Again?' I asked, aghast.

'Always falling off the monkey bridge, he is. Right, get up, Bobby, and go and help Tommy with some whittling.'

On that command, Bobby snapped out of his unconsciousness, leapt from the bike and scurried away into the tents.

'Sorry about that. Can I offer you some tea?' He then looked about mischievously. 'Or would you prefer some grog?'

'Grog'd be nice,' I said, and the able seaman led me into his tent.

'This lot are one of the finest bunch of Sea Scouts ever to inflate a dinghy,' he said, as he pulled a small flask from under his bunk.

The tent was decorated with lots of photos of the

able seaman. And his scouts. And some badges. And some awards.

He placed a couple of cups on a table. 'One tot or two?'

'Just the one,' I replied.

He poured the drinks, then pointed to a badge on his arm.

'See that? Crow's-nest Operative – advanced,' he said proudly.

'Very nice,' I said, slurping. Why was he telling me this?

'You're probably wondering why I'm telling you this.'

I shifted uncomfortably.

'I got this badge for being observant – and do you know what I've just observed?'

'No . . .'

'I observed that you, too, have a nautical something about you!'

'I do, I do!' I said, leaping to my feet. 'I am Sam Hawkins, Pirate Detective. You've probably heard of me.'

'Probably have. Just remind me . . .'

'Sam Hawkins, Pirate Detective, the finest detective ever to swash a buckle. I've cut and thrust my way across the seven seas. I've smuggled clams with the best of 'em!'

'I bet you've got many a salty tale to tell, eh?' he asked.

'I have, I have! There was the time Congo Ali and I were wedged between the keel of the good ship *Scuttle Butt* and the *Giddy Kipper*—'

'Wait a minute!'

He suddenly disappeared outside and I heard shouting.

'Fall in, Sea Scouts – 1 . . . 2 . . . 3 . . . 4! 1 . . . 2 . . . 3 . . . 4!'

This was followed by the sound of hundreds of pairs of feet tramping over to the tent. I put my ear closer to the canvas.

'Now, today we have a very special treat, Sea Scouts. We have a guest here – an experienced seaman . . .'

The crowded Sea Scouts all went 'Oooo' in expectation.

'In fact, a pirate . . .'

This got a bigger 'Ooooo!'

'In fact, a pirate detective . . .'

This got the biggest 'Ooooo!!' of all.

'So give a hearty yo-ho-ho to Sam Hawkins!'

'Yo-ho-ho!' they all yelled, and clapped loudly.

I poked my head out of the tent. I must have looked like a porpoise emerging from coral.

All their little eyes were gazing at me. I stepped out

27

and cleared my throat. Where to start? Which of all my nautical tales could I thrill them with? I took a deep breath and began.

'The day I was lashed to a cannon and made to eat my own bellybutton fluff was a day I shall remember for a very long time . . .'

And so I launched into a well-worn tale that I had recited on many occasions. 'Twas a grand tale – a little excitement, a little sadness, a little laughter, a little penguin. I knew this story so well that, as my mouth chatted away, my mind wandered. And as it wandered, it wondered.

I gazed down at the enthralled faces before me. Some were so enthralled they'd started to talk among themselves; others were so enthralled they'd started playing tig.

I noticed each and every Sea Scout had a pouch on his belt. A rather large pouch, in fact. Whatever could be kept in a pouch that size, I wondered.

And then the anchor dropped! My lightning brain put it all together. 'Twas brilliant! 'Twas obvious! These rapscallion Sea Scouts had toppled the Pointy Head Lighthouse with one of their scouty contraptions. The lighthouse had fallen with a deafening crunch. A crunch as witnessed by Billy Buddy's ears. Then – I couldn't believe the audacity of their plan – they had swarmed across the collapsed building, stuffing bricks in their pouches. And I'd bet my sea-bottom dollar that those bricks were still in those pouches! I, Sam Hawkins, had solved the case. Ha!

I stopped mid-sentence and looked at the shoal of faces before me.

'Think you're clever, eh?' I said.

Those who were still listening seemed confused by this twist in the tale. The tigging stopped and they started to pay attention.

'Think you could get away with it, eh?'

The able seaman looked about, a little confused.

'Did you think no one would notice?' I continued. 'That was the finest lighthouse ever to shine out to sea. 'Twas the home of Billy Buddy! And you call yourself Sea Scouts!'

The scouts started to look at each other for some sort of explanation. They were faking their innocence very convincingly, I thought. Perhaps they'd got a badge in it.

'I accuse you of stealing the Pointy Head Lighthouse!' I declared, pointing at as many of them as I could in one go.

There was some muttering among them. Able Seaman Wave was stunned by the accusation.

One of the scouts, the smallest one, was pushed forward and asked very clearly, 'But where would we put it?'

'Ha! Do these look like blind man's eyes! Those pouches you have on your belt are the self-same size as the bricks that made up the lighthouse. You each have a brick in your pouch.'

They suddenly all chorused in unison, 'No, we don't!'

'What?'

'We haven't got any bricks in our pouches!'

I held my ground.

'Prove it. Empty your pouches!'

And then the tide turned. Able Seaman Wave lined up his scouts and ordered them to follow my instruction. String, plasters, catapults, Gameboys, yo-yos, boiled sweets – all in turn were produced from the pouches.

I stumbled along the ranks inspecting the contents.

Jellyfish! Not one lighthouse brick emerged. Curses and cuttlefish!

The Sea Scouts gazed at me.

I gazed back. I shuffled slightly and then said, 'Anyway, back to the story . . .'

At this, the entire crowd rose like a wave and started to charge towards me, yelling something unintelligible.

For the splittiest of split seconds, I thought about standing my ground. But I had a good pair of sea legs and decided to put them to use. I legged it. I tore towards the Nippy Clipper, threw myself aboard and swiftly kick-started it into life. The engine roared and I sped through the gate of the field and on to the road.

I sighed a relieved sigh, revved the engine and droved rapidly away. 'Twas at this point I noticed something was missing. I looked about. Where were all my toilet rolls?

Stretched across the road ahead was a strange contraption. 'Twas a rope bridge. And standing on the rope bridge were the Sea Scouts. And each Sea Scout was armed with a toilet roll.

I screeched to a halt. The scouts glared at me. Should I risk humiliation and failure by riding under the bridge back to Washed-upon-the-Beach? Or should I ride in the opposite direction, taking the longer route to avoid a deluge of toilet rolls?

'Twas a difficult decision to make, I thought, as I rode off in the opposite direction.

Chapter Three

Pah! Cod and cuttlefish! I clicked my knuckles in frustration as I ambled up the pathway of the Naughty Lass. Not one single clue had my beady eye spied. 'Twas turning into a mystery that was both intriguing and a tiny bit annoying. I mean, how am I supposed to solve a mystery without clues, for Neptune's sake? I was, quite simply, clueless.

I was just about to board my house when I was greeted by an odd happening. Before my salty palm could clutch the knob, the door was flung open and out burst my old muckers, Lan Ho and Molly. Fluttering above them was Spot the Parrot. I rubbed my weary eyes. Did he really have a paper hat on his little feathered head? I glanced at Ho and Molly. They, too, were wearing paper hats. Newspaper hats, in fact. Whatever was a-going on?

'Congratulations, big boss!' announced Lan Ho

proudly. 'You got a new case to solve. So we've decided to celebrate and bake you a cake!'

I knew Ho's cooking from personal experience. I still take the pills. I was touched by the gesture of support from my crew, though. Molly gave me a thumbs-up and kissed the top of my head. Spot, playfully, tugged at my neckerchief and Ho produced the cake. 'Twas a green one.

'Green cake, my favourite,' I lied. 'What . . . what . . . flavour is it?'

Ho beamed. 'Sea-sponge and spinach!'

'How exotic,' I said, as he sliced a piece and Molly held the plate.

'And I chopped the onions!' she said.

I held the slice of green cake in my hand and gazed at it. How could I disappoint old Ho after all the trouble he'd been to? He was the worst cook ever to stir-fry custard, but his little face smiled winningly at me. I braced myself and opened my mouth to bite.

'Tell us about the case, boss!' he said eagerly, and Spot clapped his wings excitedly.

'Ah, 'twill prove a slimy, grimy tale, me maties! I've run my seagull eye across the scene of the crime and examined the place from fore to aft. Not one single, solitary clue has come over the horizon.'

Spot stopped clapping.

'What?' said Ho, in the middle of eating a slice.

'What?' said Molly, in the middle of eating the rest of the cake.

I shifted uncomfortably from foot to foot.

'No clue has hove into view!'

'You haven't found any clues?' said Molly, wiping her lips.

I hesitated, but had to come clean. 'No clues.'

And with that, Ho snatched the slice of cake from my hand, turned and stomped into the house. Molly brushed the crumbs from her hands, flicked both my ears and joined him. Spot gave my nose a sharp peck and followed the fleet inside. I was about to do the same when the door was slammed in my face.

I slumped on the doorstep, muttering nautical curses. Then a jolly thought entered my brain. At least I wouldn't have to eat Ho's cake. I giggled with glee. Then stopped giggling as a second thought entered my brain.

I'd forgotten my keys. Seaweed!

I shouted through the letter box.

'Hello! Let me in . . . Hello?'

I don't know if it's possible to break your bottom, but it felt as if I'd broken mine. I sat in the lounge of the Naughty Lass on a very soft cushion, while by my side sat Spot, nursing a mild wing wound.

My ragbag of a crew had seen fit to leave their noble leader on the doorstep so I'd had to gain entry via a different porthole. I chose the kitchen window, which was partly ajar. As I lowered my ample load over the window sill, my boot slipped on some soap. I crashed into the sink (which was filled to the gunnels with unwashed pots), banged against a saucepan, which catapulted a chopstick towards Spot, pinning him to the fridge door. I collapsed and Ho and Molly found me sitting in a wok.

So there I was with my broken bottom, my damaged parrot and my reputation as a crime-solver in tatters. I twiddled my thumbs and wondered what to do. I flicked idly through a copy of *Detecting Made Simple*. I looked at the first line: 'First, find your clues.' I hurled the book across the room and sat in a huffing silence.

At that point the ship's bell rang.

Now, I have to explain about the ship's bell. 'Twas handed down to me by my great-uncle 'Tweaker' Hawkins, one of the finest pirates ever to walk the plank. He went down in nautical history for cutting the whiskers off an infamous villain, Greenbeard the pirate. For years after, Greenbeard was known simply as Green.

Legend had it this very bell was snaffled from under the nose of the king of Spain and brought safely back to Blighty, where it became a Hawkins heirloom. And I was the last in the Hawkins line, so 'twas mine. We used it aboard the Naughty Lass to announce meetings or meals. But we didn't have a meeting planned for today and dinner was a long way off. So I couldn't understand why 'twas ringing.

Ping! went the bell.

I looked about. So did Spot.

Then once more all fell silent.

Ping!

I sat up straight.

Silence once more.

I relaxed.

Ping!!

I looked at Spot.

'Are you dinging my bell?'

Spot shook his confused little head.

Ping! it went again, and this time a peanut hit me in the eye. Peanuts? Piratical thoughts washed through my brain. A distant memory was a-stirring.

At that point Ho shouted from upstairs.

'Boss, there's a man at the door with a funny face. Shall I tell him you've already got one?'

Man with a funny face? Bells ringing? Peanuts? It couldn't be, could it?

I jumped to my feet and, holding my broken bottom, hurried to the front door. I stopped and heard a sound that confirmed my suspicions. 'Twas a sea shanty.

'With a yo and a ho and a yo-yo-ho, I'll spit on your granny for tuppence!'

I threw open the door.

'Long John Saliva!' I cried.

And, indeed, 'twas he. The lanky buccaneer from my merry days at sea. This was the man who could spit a peanut 100 metres with deadly accuracy. 'Twas he who'd rung my bell. He'd been spitting peanuts through the letter box.

'Seasick Sam Hawkins!' he cried back.

We threw ourselves into our old foot-wagging greeting as if 'twere yesterday. I led him inside.

Good old Long John Saliva!

'I thought you'd gone to a watery grave years ago!' I said, dinging the bell to gather my crew.

'No, no! 'Twas but a rumour I put about.' He threw himself into the comfy settee and smacked the arm with jollity. A cloud of dust arose and I wafted it with my hat.

'Seems old "Jelly-belly" Hawkins has done himself proud!' he said, doffing his cap to the parrot.

Spot shrugged his good wing in response.

Ho and Molly ambled into the room and

looked at our new guest cautiously.

'Crew, this is Long John Saliva, an old briny buddy of mine. You've heard me mention his name many a time!'

'No, we haven't,' said Ho, shaking Long John's hand.

Molly inflicted a hug.

'Go shake a jolly cocktail to welcome our guest while we chat about old times.'

Ho and Molly took to their task and Long John and I set sail on a tale-telling voyage, stirring and whirling stories from our piratical past. So many tales washed by: the day Long John and I were caught helping ourselves to the Golden Turtle of Dim Sum by the Chinese pirate Dip Toh; the time Long John rescued me from the evil clutches of Skipper 'Kipper' Whipper, just as I was about to be keel-hauled; the fortnight we spent in a treasure chest, waiting to surprise the Flinkle Twins – pity we'd buried ourselves on the wrong island!

The time . . . oh, I could go on. But those times were gone. And here we were, washed up in Washed-upon-the-Beach like two pieces of lost driftwood.

I looked at my old pal. He hadn't changed a bit. In fact, I don't think he'd changed his socks either. One of the finest mutineers with whom I'd ever shared a tot, that man. We pirates stick together. I'd do anything for the old salt.

'So what brings you to the old Naughty Lass, eh, Long John?'

'I need to borrow some money—'

'Well, it's been lovely meeting you again,' I said, pushing him into the hall. 'Do drop by another— '

'All right, all right, all right!' he cried, pushing away my pushes and clutching his bag of peanuts to his chest. 'If you can't lend an old mucker some dosh, maybe you could put me up for the night?'

Ho stood in the kitchen doorway with two bubbling cocktails.

'Guest, Ho!'

'I'll put a duvet in the bath!' he said, and ran upstairs.

It seemed that my old maritime mate had turned his back on pirating and taken up another profession. He'd formed a rock band called Long John Saliva and the Spittoons. I'd heard him play air-guitar, made from real hair, and was mightily impressed. Seems he'd been booked to play at the Rockness Monster Rock Festival. This was an annual event here in Washed-upon-the-Beach and 'twas known throughout the globe as the finest gathering of sea-shantiers. Not only was it famous for its music, but every year at the Rockness Monster Rock Festival the legendary

Rockness Monster appeared. It was a strange, dark shadow form. No one knew where it came from or where it disappeared to, but no festival was complete without it – and, of course, all the accompanying Rockness Monster merchandising.

So, 'twas a major event in Washed-upon-the-Beach's cultural calendar. Money would soon come flooding in for Long John, but for the time being he was as skint as a clam. Still, we had tales to tell. We plunged late into the night with our tale-telling marathon. Ho and Molly had excused themselves and gone to bed. But Long John and I had leagues yet to cover.

I slurped another cocktail.

'And the time you hid an eel in your hat!' I giggled.

'Eel in my hat, yes, that was a good one.'

Long John stood up. He was a tall, thin fellow. Could do with a good bit of fodder, I thought. 'Twas clear he had fallen on hard times.

'I need to visit the bilge room!'

I sat up.

'Of course, second on the left at the top of the stairs.'

Long John strode from the room.

Well, well, who would have thought it? Old Long John Saliva! 'Twas a delight to see his weathered face. But I couldn't stop thoughts of my current case flooding into my brain.

A stolen lighthouse and no clues. Nothing but Billy Buddy's story – which reminded me. Who is Harvey Clump? I must look into that in the morning.

'Twas at this point I looked down at the wonky coffee table.

I rubbed my weary eyes.

There on the table, next to a pile of peanuts, was a paper aeroplane. And it hadn't been there before. How odd! I leaned over and inspected it. I glanced at the open window. Must have come through there. Scurrying across, I looked up and down the dark and empty Puddle Lane. Not a solitary sole could I see.

I scratched my head and returned to my armchair. I took up my squeeze-box and softly squeezed out a shanty.

'There's a crab at the bottom of the ocean,' I sang, as Long John returned, 'and his name is—'

'What's that?' said Long John, pointing at the note.

'Just a paper plane – probably the kids next door up to no good. They're always throwing things over the fence or poking things through the letter box.'

Long John fingered the plane and slowly unfolded it.

'Well, pickle my herrings. Look at that!'

He handed me the paper. I gazed at it. There, scrawled in spidery writing, was the following:

Sam Hawkins

I have the **Pointy Head** lighthouse.
If you ever want to see it again
I require **gold** — and lots of it.

The Scarlet Winkle.
X

I read the note again.

'Scarlet Winkle? Who's the Scarlet Winkle?'

'Never heard of him,' said Long John, draining his cocktail and innocently running his finger along my sea-shell shelf.

'And what's this?' I asked Long John, peering closer.

There, on the edge of the note, was a clear and unmistakable indentation.

'No idea!'

I danced a little hornpipe.

'I might not know who the lighthouse-napper is, but I do know one thing,' I giggled.

Long John stopped and looked at me.

'What do you know?' he asked.

'I know that I've got my first clue!'

I gave a triumphant slurp on my cocktail.

Chapter Four

The next morning I ambled down the stairs and shuffled into the living room. The place was festooned with nuts of all shapes and sizes. I rubbed my eyes and tried to recall the events of the previous evening. I groaned at the memory – the spitting contest.

At about three bells, and after a number of grogs, I had encouraged Long John Saliva to demonstrate his talents. I supplied him with a plentiful supply of nuts and seeds, and we spat and gobbed till the early hours. 'Twas like days gone by. And what a spitter was Long John – his nickname was well earned. He could spit a peanut at a light switch and turn it on, he could close a door by propelling a walnut and he could put out a windowpane with an avocado stone. He could even dial the speaking clock with a selection of sunflower seeds.

I surveyed the debris and sighed. Time to start cleaning.

I heard Ho and Molly stirring and soon they were bounding downstairs, singing a merry sea shanty. 'Twas unusual for them to be so happy at this early hour.

They bounded into the living room.

They saw the mess.

They bounded out. Pah!

They bounded back in again carrying a vacuum cleaner.

Aha! What a noble pair of naval skivvies. They were going to clean up my mess for me.

They handed me the vacuum cleaner and bounded out of the room.

Puddle water!

I cleaned the Naughty Lass living room from bow to stern and made a jolly job of it too. Sam Hawkins has cleaned up bigger messes than this. Wasn't it me who single-handedly scrubbed the entire deck of *The Galloping Doodoo* in two hours flat? 'Twas a proud moment for me as the captain, Two-tongue Tessie, inspected my work, slipped on a bar of soap and fell in a barrel. We laughed about it later as she locked me in the brig.

I stamped on the start button and the vacuum

cleaner roared like a hungry dolphin. I grabbed the hose part as if it were a sword and began poking it into every nook and cranny throughout the room. As I merrily set about my chore, I heard something a-groaning. I stamped the machine off.

The groaning continued. My detecting ear led me to the settee and I carefully peered behind it. Suddenly, in an eruption of naughty nautical curses, Long John Saliva surged out like a performing whale. His face resembled a turtle's bottom. Two red eyes were peering out from above his thick black, grey and blue beard. He spat out a ball of fluff and another rude word. So this is what Long John Saliva looks like first thing in the morning. Not the prettiest of sights.

'Stop that blightering noise. I'm a-trying to sleep!' he announced in a croaky voice, and then disappeared behind the settee again.

I crept out to fetch a dustpan and brush.

I thought a hearty dollop of Ho's cooking might swill out our guest's aching brain. And indeed it did.

'What in the darkest depths of the deep is that?' he said, spitting the first mouthful through the window and into the dustbin outside.

Ho stared at Long John and said, 'It's deep-fried raspberry yoghurt and parsley. I made it up!'

'Made it up? I nearly threw it up! Are you trying to kill me, little boy?'

He waved the butter knife at Ho. I quelled his anger with a well-aimed witty salvo.

'On guard!'

I produced my own breakfast knife and we engaged in a pretend duel across the table.

'Just like the old days, eh, Long John?'

Ho huffingly removed Long John's plate and tossed the contents into the bin. He wiped his hands and left the room stroppily.

He almost collided with Molly as she stomped into the room clutching a copy of this month's *Ahoy!* magazine.

'Who's done this?' she bellowed.

'Twas a bellow that fell harshly on our sleep-deprived ears. I leapt in surprise and Long John almost sliced off my ear with his butter knife. We turned to Molly.

'Well?' she snarled, and lumbered towards us like a disgruntled hippo.

She was holding up the magazine. On the cover was a picture of Helen Highwater, the beautiful film star, but she looked a little different from how I remembered her. I peered closer. She had no eyes. She had no mouth either. There was a hole where each should be. A hole about the size of a peanut. Oh dear.

'She's my favourite!'

'Sorry about that, Molly, my old mate. We needed a bit of target practice and that magazine came to hand!'

Molly bent across the breakfast table and flicked my ears. I hate it when she does that.

'Don't flick my ears in front of our guest!'

At that she leaned over and flicked Long John's ears. And then she stomped from the room, hugging the magazine to her chest.

And she almost collided with Spot, who fluttered in carrying his seed tray in his little beak. He landed on the table, scuttled over to Long John and emptied the contents before him. Among his usual diet of bird-seed was a small collection of cashew nuts. He rolled his eyes and tutted, then flew from the room.

'What a tempestuous, tantrum-throwing gaggle of hot-heads!' Long John finally said. 'I wouldn't trust 'em as far as I could spit 'em!'

I started tapping into my boiled egg. 'And you should see them when they're angry . . .'

Later that day Long John and I were walking along the dockside at Washed-upon-the-Beach and chatting. Slowly our naval parley turned towards the case on which I was currently embarked.

'Sounds odd!' said Long John, tugging at his beard.

'I mean, how do you steal a lighthouse?' I asked, turning to him.

Over his shoulder I could see a large crane loading long, thick pipes aboard a tanker.

I gazed up at it and pondered the impossible task of snaffling off with an item such as a lighthouse. The crane loaded pipe after pipe aboard the tanker. Pipe after pipe. I shook myself from my pondering and said, 'Well, I'm not going to find any clues stood a-standing here!'

And on we walked.

Suddenly an idea occurred to Long John.

'Maybe the lighthouse was dismantled brick by brick and hidden somewhere. Maybe a well-trained platoon of sailors or—'

I silenced him with a wave of my hand.

'No, no. I've already investigated that particular avenue. And I lost 100 toilet rolls in the process. Hmm, 'tis a tanglesome teaser. But at least we now have a clue!'

I pulled the ransom note from my pocket and flattened it out. The indentation was still there. Perhaps this itself was a clue. Long John peered closely at it. Then a smile swam across his chops.

'Tooth marks!' he declared.

I wasn't sure what he meant.

'I know exactly what you mean!' I said, starting to put away the note.

Long John grabbed it from me.

'That's it, my old deck-swabber. Whoever wrote this note left a tell-tale tooth mark on it. Ha!'

Long John looked at the note, then he slowly turned and gazed at my teeth. A strange, quizzical look came into his eyes.

I quickly put the note in my mouth and bit a corner. 'At least I'm innocent – my teeth make a different sort of mark!' I waggled the note before Long John's eyes.

'Twas not meant to be a funny thing to say, but suddenly Long John started to laugh, and when he laughs his eyebrows wiggle like two caterpillars doing a salsa dance.

'That's it!' he chuckled.

'That's it!' I echoed, not having a clue what he was talking about.

He jabbed a finger at the tooth mark.

'Whoever's teeth fit that mark must be the culprit!'

'That's it!' I shouted, a little surer now. Of course, 'twas a simple but devious ploy. 'All we need to do is ask people to bite into a piece of paper, and whoever's bite matches these marks is the slimy serpent we seek!'

'Simple!' whooped Long John.

'Where shall we begin?' I whooped back delightly.

'With your hot-headed crew!'

'Oh . . . . . .'

And so we returned to the Naughty Lass.

'Now then, crew!' said Long John, pacing up and down in front of my ranked crew, 'I don't want you to feel you're being accused of anything.'

'Oh, no, no,' I added.

'In fact, we're convinced you are completely innocent.'

'Innocent!' I repeated. Whose case was this anyway?

'So we need to prove your innocence.'

He whipped a blank piece of paper from his tunic and handed it to Ho.

'Bite into that, would you?' Ho dutifully followed his orders. I tried to lighten the situation with a quip.

'Taste nice, does it?'

Ho handed back the bitten sheet. 'Better than my cooking apparently!' he said sarcastically.

But the comment was washed aside as both Long John and I compared Ho's tooth marks to the one on the ransom note. We finally agreed.

'Nope!'

Next we moved on to Spot, who was quietly

perched on Molly's shoulder.

'Now you, Mr Parrot!' said Long John, poking the paper towards Spot's beak.

He nibbled a corner and the evidence was examined.

'Nope!'

He moved on to the final crew member, Molly.

'But I'm a detective,' she moaned.

'Detective assistant!' I corrected her.

'I don't commit crimes! I solve them!'

'*Help* solve them,' I added.

'Hmm, good cover for a criminal,' said Long John. 'A detective who commits crimes while appearing to solve them!'

'Twasn't the wisest of things to say to Molly. She lurched forward and raised her hands towards Long John's ears.

'What are you implying?'

'Molly, don't injure our guest!' I ordered.

Her anger subsided and she fell back into line.

'Just bite, Moll, there's a good girl.'

She snatched the paper from Long John, made a mark and handed it back.

As she mumbled about her innocence and the unfairness of it all, Long John and I held the paper to the light.

A dry gulp tugged at my throat.

Long John turned and a sneaky smirk poked out from under his beard. It couldn't be true!

'A perfect match!' he announced quietly.

'Twas not the easiest of tasks getting Molly into the police car. Long John Saliva and officers Stump and Stibbins tugged and hugged, and pushed and pulled, and screamed and shouted. Eventually, with the promise of cake, she was lured into the back seat and the door was locked.

But 'twas a wasted effort, I thought. I looked down from my bedroom window as the police duh-duhed into the distance. Molly was as innocent as a tadpole. She'd never break the law. She might have bent it in two on occasions, but never, never broken it.

I wandered past her old room, where Long John was quickly unpacking his bags and making himself at home. I padded downstairs and into the living room. Ho was sitting in a fuming silence and Spot sat on his head with his wings folded.

"Twill not be for long, me old pals. 'Tis obviously some mistake. Maybe she has similar teeth to some vile villain. Maybe her molars are of the selfsame layout as those of the criminal who stole the lighthouse! What do you say, maties?'

I can't tell you what they said, partly because it's

rude and partly because I can't spell some of it. But 'twas obvious they were displeased. Ho stomped from the room and Spot fluttered off with an attitude.

What could I do? I was washed into a corner.

I slumped into an armchair and grabbed the TV guide.

'*Good Mooring with Tom, Dick and Harriet*. That'll take me weary mind off things,' I said as I stabbed the remote.

A picture shimmered into view. 'Twas one of those shiny television studios made to look like a living room though it isn't really one. A bright and shiny face beamed out, pleading to be liked.

'Hello!' it said. 'Today we're interviewing the Mayor of Washed-upon-the-Beach, Lola Schwartz . . .'

I sat up straight. I knew her. She'd given me my Golden Albatross – the highest honour a landlubber could have.

'. . . and quadrillionaire businessman, Harvey Clump.'

There on the settee next to the Mayor sat a well-groomed man with finely cut hair and an expensive suit covering his strapping body. This was a go-getter businessman who'd gone and got. Harvey Clump? That name rang a distant ship's bell.

The conversation dribbled through nonsense about haircare products and suchlike, but then my ears pricked up. The man Clump made an announcement.

'Yes, that's right!' he said. 'Today is a special day, as I am announcing the line-up for this year's Rockness Monster Rock Festival, which I am personally sponsoring!'

'And will the famous Rockness Monster be making its usual appearance?' asked the interviewer, smiling.

Clump laughed.

'What festival would be complete without it?'

'Tell us a little about the Rockness Monster!'

Clump looked bashful, or at least tried to. 'Well, it's a mystery, really. Every year at the festival the monster appears from out of the darkness and then simply disappears! No one knows any more than that!' He winked broadly at the camera. 'And the main attraction in the arena this year will be the famous Pointy Head Lighthouse!'

The interviewer slickly intervened. 'Tell us a little about that.'

Clump oozed answers, but I heard no more as my thoughts had begun to drift away. On the screen now was an artist's impression of what the festival stadium would look like. If that picture was correct, they were planning to build it on the headland where the lighthouse had once stood. Did they know? Did they know the lighthouse was no longer there? Then a darker thought washed into my piratical mind. Did Clump take the lighthouse? Maybe for publicity? A thousand questions eddied through my brain. Of course, Harvey Clump was a name that had crossed the threshold of my ears only very recently. Billy Buddy had mentioned it and, if I recalled correctly, swiftly hushed himself up. It was obvious that Billy Buddy knew more than either of him was letting on. This was becoming an intriguing little case and one I was determined to solve.

'Twould seem the next port into which I should drop my anchor was the Red Sea Lion Tavern.

Chapter Five

'Twas a bright and cheery day in Washed-upon-the-Beach as I strutted along the main street. Old Sam Hawkins was, once more, piloting his ship through high adventure. It had been a long time since my nautical brain had wrestled with a slippery puzzle such as this, but I was determined 'twould be solved and the culprits brought to jolly justice.

I whistled a breezy sea shanty and saw a sign up ahead that put a spring in my step:

RED SEA LION TAVERN

And underneath it said:

**FOOD SERVED ALL DAY
TRY OUR KIPPERS
YOU WON'T GET BETTER!**

A splendid old place was the Red Sea Lion Tavern. Finest place ever to quench a thirst. In days gone by 'twas where many a weary sailor would hang his hat and quaff a grog or two. Oh, the hours I've spent here regaling piratical pals with tales of my seafaring life. I hadn't been inside for many a year, though, and I wondered if my old pal Zanzibar Stan still ran it.

I was a little early for opening time, so I poked the doorbell and I heard a tinkling inside.

A few seconds later the door opened and there stood my old pal. We called him Zanzibar because it rhymed with Stan the Bar. They called me Samziprat. I never found out why.

'Yo-ho-ho!' I chortled my greeting. ''Tis your old pal Sam Hawkins, pirate adventurer.'

Stan was as round as the barrels from which he served. He had a jolly face, but on it was a sour expression. Perhaps he hadn't recognized me.

'Sam Hawkins!' I nodded encouragingly. 'Champion of the high seas and darling of the ladies.'

Nothing. Not a tinkle of recognition.

'And now Sam Hawkins, Pirate Detective, righter of wrongs!'

This had taken the wind out of my sails a little. Didn't he recognize his old tot-swigging mate?

'Sam Hawkins who once leapt the gaping gap between the *Scuttle Butt* and *The Gutless Wonder* to save Bearded Barbara from a sloppy, sloshy death? I was the talk of the town that night!'

'I know who you are!' he said finally. He had a voice like a depressed crab. 'You are Sam Hawkins, who could chase customers from my tavern within seconds of opening his mouth!'

I was taken aback.

'Sam Hawkins, tall-tale teller!' he continued.

Tall-tale teller? But I'm only five foot seven.

'Sam Hawkins, the dullest of bores!'

'I'm not! Take it back!'

'For years you bored the pints off my customers!' he said. 'And you still owe me forty-two pounds from five years ago!'

'Oh, yes,' I said, 'that night with the Cockle Triplets. Dear, dear. Yes, you've got me there, old governor. I shall write you a cheque forthwith.'

He stepped back and allowed me into the tavern.

I dutifully scrolled my signature across a Dogger Bank cheque and handed it across the bar.

'There!' I said, and smiled.

'Now what do you want?' he said, holding it up to the light.

'I'll have a Clam Tipple, if you're offering!' I said gleefully.

Zanzibar Stan leaned across the bar and looked into my eyes.

'I'm not serving you any drinks. It takes me about five years to get paid. Have you come here with a purpose?'

I was confuddled by his question.

'Have I come here with a porpoise? I didn't know I had to bring one. I might have a pilchard somewhere!'

I was starting to search through my pockets when Stan grabbed me by my neckerchief and pulled me across the bar. A couple of tankards toppled in my wake. He spoke very slowly and very loudly in my shell-like.

'What . . . do . . . you . . . want?'

He released me and I slumped on a bar stool.

'I'd like to speak to Billy Buddy, please, if I may, thank you!'

'Top of the stairs, turn right, room 6!'

I rapped loudly on the door of room 6. There was no answer, but from inside I heard bickering. I put my ear to the keyhole.

'You answer it!'

'Why should I?'

'You don't do much else!'

'How dare you!'

Cod's roe! Billy Buddy was having another argument with himself. Finally the door was opened and there stood the sprouty-faced fellow.

'Come in!' he said, and I found myself in the poky little hold that passed for his accommodation. 'Twas a dark and damp room with a single bed, a single tap, a single lamp and a single settee.

Billy Buddy sat on the small settee. It creaked slightly.

'Nice place!' I said encouragingly.

'Not as nice as my old lighthouse.'

'Perhaps not,' I said, running my finger along the dust-ridden window sill.

'*Offer our guest a seat, then!*' said his second voice, and he moved further up the settee and patted the space he'd left.

I sat by him.

'All I have now is my memories,' he said, stifling a tear, and slid a suitcase from under the bed.

Two clicks and 'twas open. He thrust a photo album at me.

'This is one of me and Bessie the bulb. Here I am washing the windows. This is one of me climbing my ladder and here I am next to the lighthouse doorstep . . .'

He had a wodge of photos in this album. 'Twas as thick as a ship's log after a particularly harrowing adventure.

'Very nice,' I said. 'Who took the photographs?'

'*Me, of course!*' he replied in his second voice.

I thought about that for a moment, but it made my head hurt, so I quickly changed the subject.

'When last we met, my old mate, you mentioned a name.'

'Did I?'

'I didn't!'

'You did!'

'Oh, yes, I did, didn't ?!'

'Well, don't mention it again.'

'But he's going to find out eventually!'

'All right, you tell him. But if you get in trouble, don't come running to me!'

This short dialogue was conducted by Billy Buddy swivelling back and forth on the settee, changing his voice with each swivel.

'I believe 'twas Harvey Clump!' I said, softly reeling in my catch.

'Harvey Clump – quadrillionaire businessman, you mean!'

'That's the happy chappie! What part does he play in this mystery, pray!'

'Well, there's not much to tell really. He came to see us the other day and told us all about building the Rockness Monster Rock Festival stadium and how he'd like to buy our lighthouse. We refused, of course. We've lived at Pointy Head Lighthouse far too long to think about moving.'

He pulled a handkerchief from his dungaree pocket, blew his nose and patted himself on the shoulder.

'Be brave!' he said gently.

'*Thank you.*' He continued his tale. '*So he went off on his way and the next thing we know the lighthouse had vanished without a trace!*'

I scratched my grizzled chin and pondered. Could it be that Harvey Clump had stolen the lighthouse so he could build his rock stadium without any hassle from the lighthouse's resident? And if so, what was the evidence? And if he had stolen it, why was a ransom note sent? And by whom? I suddenly snapped out of my dreamy thinking as I heard Billy Buddy saying, '. . . Rockness Monster ever again.'

'*Shh!*' he hushed himself.

'What did you say?' I inquired.

'*Don't say a word!*' Billy cautioned himself with a pointing finger.

'He's bound to find out sooner or later. He's a detective.'

'He's right, you know! Go on!' I said.

Billy shrugged and sat back in the settee.

'Every year since the festival began *we* have been the monster.'

'What?'

I couldn't believe this. The Rockness Monster was shrouded in secrecy. No one knew anything about it, or so I thought. I looked at the little man as he continued his tale.

'For years the Pointy Head Lighthouse keepers have been in charge of making the monster appear.'

I was scratching my head in confusion. 'But how?'

And with this question Billy Buddy turned on the small lamp by the settee and pointed it at the damp wall. I was befuddled by his behaviour but remained patient. Billy clasped his two hands together.

'Put your thumb up!' he ordered himself.

'*That is my thumb!*' he responded. '*Wiggle your little finger!*'

'I am!' he snapped back.

When he was finally in agreement with himself, he slowly slid his hands into the beam of the lamp. And there, silhouetted on the wall of this tatty room, was the shadowy outline known to everyone in Washed-upon-the-Beach as the Rockness Monster.

I almost gurgled with delight.

'You do the Rockness Monster!' I shouted.

'Yes! Every year. But without the Pointy Head Lighthouse and Beaming Bessie, the Rockness Monster is no more!' He changed his hands into the shape of a bird and it flew away.

'*Oh, that was pretty!*'

'Thank you.'

Billy switched off the light as I pondered these thoughts. He pulled another memento from his suitcase. A miniature lighthouse.

'Do you like it? We made it ourselves.'

'Twas very nice, a perfect reproduction of the Pointy Head Lighthouse, but I had no time for this now. I had a slippery eel to grill.

'*We used to make models of things.*'

'This was our favourite!'

He held up a small duster. A model duster, in fact.

'*Would you like to help us clean it?*'

I started reversing towards the door.

'No, no, thank you – maybe next time. I have other fish to fry!'

And with those words I was through the door, down the stairs and on to the street at a rare rate of knots.

Now to track down Harvey Clump.

I moored the Nippy Clipper to a lamppost outside the grand and mighty skyscraper known as Clump Tower. As I did, a fascinating sight met my eyes.

A long, sleek and black limo sat resplendent outside. Huddled around it was a gaggle of photographers snapping shots of the car.

'Twas like watching a shoal of piranha nibbling the carcass of a whale.

As I walked towards the crowd, the doors of Clump Tower slid slowly aside and there stood the man himself – Harvey Clump, quadrillionaire and, if my nautical mind suspected correctly, thief of the Pointy Head Lighthouse.

He was surrounded by a group of tubby thugs in dark suits and sunglasses who plunged into the crowd and tried to forge a route from the door to the car. 'Twas not an easy task, for as soon as the glistening features of the businessman hove into view, the crowd surged like a mighty wave. The photographers flashed and the reporters yelled questions about the Rockness Monster Rock Festival.

I launched myself into the throng.

'Sam Hawkins, *Daily Squid*!' I shouted, trying to pass myself off as a journalist and get some answers. 'Do you know the whereabouts of the lost lighthouse?' But my words were drowned in an ocean of chatter.

Harvey Clump waved majestically as he made his way to his limo, but answered no questions. He climbed in and the door was slammed shut.

I had to think fast. I looked back and forth and my beady eye fell upon the sunroof. 'Twould be an easy task to slide over the boot and poke my head through it.

I extracted myself from the snapping and chattering crowd and made my way to the rear of the vehicle. I hastily looked about and climbed on the boot. The thugs hadn't spotted me and so I crawled on to the roof.

At this point I heard the engine start. 'Twas then I realized I hadn't thought this through.

Before I could throw myself overboard, the limo was pulling away from the kerb. I grasped on to the radio aerial and gulped a terrified gulp.

As the limo drove along the street, it started to gain speed. I could feel the wind in my hair and the butterflies in my stomach.

But there was no way out. I glanced at the pavement as it flew past. I had to make a decision. Should I bail out or finish my task?

I took a deep breath, hiccuped, and started to make for the sunroof. The sea gods were smiling on me – it was open.

I eased back the glass just enough to poke in my head.

'Hello!' I said, dangling upside down into the car. 'Sam Hawkins, *Daily Squid* . . .'

Inside, Harvey Clump was stabbing at a calculator in one hand and jabbering into a mobile phone in the other. He dropped both as I spoke. He looked up at my face. I tried to smile winningly, but lost.

'Just a few questions, if you don't mind! Oops, pass me my hat, would you?'

Harvey Clump slowly passed me my old maritime hat, which had fallen off. He shook his head and emerged from his daze.

'What in the holiest of hecks are you doing on my limo?' he shouted.

'I wanted to ask about the Pointy Head Lighthouse . . . Oww!'

We'd just gone over a speed bump at speed.

Harvey continued to stare at me.

'Pass me my hat again, would you?'

Harvey snarled at me.

'Get off my limo. Don't you dare scratch the paint-work!'

'The Pointy Head Lighthouse, where is it?'

The American quadrillionaire was frantically trying to deal with this bizarre situation. He wasn't the only one.

'What are you talking about? The Pointy Head Lighthouse is the central attraction of the new Rockness Monster Rock Festival stadium. We're building around it!'

'So you wouldn't need to knock it down?'

'No!'

'Or steal it?'

'No! Look.' He unfurled the plans of the stadium and held them up for me. 'You see. The lighthouse is right in the middle and we're building—' He suddenly stopped himself. 'What am I doing? I'm sharing business secrets with a man dangling from my sunroof.'

He leaned over and rapped on the window betwixt him and the driver.

'Casey! Stop the car!'

And with that, the speeding limo screeched to a stop.

Now there's an interesting twist in the mystery, I thought, as I bounced off the pavement.

Harvey Clump opened his car door, threw my hat at me, slammed it shut and sped away.

I wafted away the fumes and sat quietly on the pavement, gathering my thoughts and the contents of my pockets.

So if Harvey Clump didn't steal the lighthouse, who did?

Chapter Six

The grimy, grey prison door clanged against the wall as Officer Stump pushed it open and stood back to let us pass. The clang echoed down the long, shadowy corridor and we shuffled through.

With a creak she closed the door behind us. I don't know whether it was her creaking or the door. Ho, Long John, Spot and I stood politely in the corridor and awaited Officer Stump's next instructions.

What a rum lot we must have looked. Long John and I had dressed ourselves splendidly in our Sunday best and little Ho had donned his finest coolie jacket, with swirling, curling golden dragons upon it. Spot was wearing his little bow-tie.

We had decided to take time from our befuddling mystery and visit our old pal Molly and jolly her along a little. I'd even brought my squeeze-box.

Officer Stump was explaining the visiting rules.

'Do not touch the prisoner, do not pass anything to the prisoner, do not take anything *from* the prisoner . . .' Her eyes fell on my squeeze-box. 'Do not sing for the prisoner.'

I'm sure she'd made up the last one, but I handed over the squeeze-box without a word.

'You can collect it from me at the end,' she said, and led us towards Molly's cell.

And what a squalid hold it was. 'Twas no more than the size of a midget's wardrobe. And a midget with very few clothes. Molly sat hunched in one corner, slurping some soup. In fact, she could sit in both corners at the same time, if you see what I mean. Watching my old boatswaining buddy in the slammer for a crime I was sure she didn't commit made my nautical blood boil. I could contain myself no longer. I ran to the bars, pressing my grizzled features against them.

'Moll, Moll, Moll! My old paddling partner, how are you? Are they treating you well? Oh, Moll, look at you – washed up in the backwaters of the local brig, with your freedom snatched from your innocent palm. I promise you, Moll, on my mother's watery grave, I'll see you set free.'

I reached out to touch her, but my tiddling arm wasn't long enough.

'Are they treating you well, Moll?'

'Very well, actually!' she said, eagerly licking the last drops of soup from her bowl.

'And how's the food?' asked Ho suspiciously.

Moll smacked her lips joyfully, but then realized she might be offending our cook.

'Terrible!' she moaned. 'Really terrible!'

She lay back on her bed and sighed.

'I miss the sea breeze, though!'

'Ha, I knew it!' I reached inside my tunic. 'I knew you'd miss the sea breeze. That's why I've brought you some.'

I withdrew a brown paper bag.

'I caught some fresh sea breeze less than twenty minutes ago.' I pushed the bag through the bars. At which point I felt a strong pain in my neck. Stump had me in a headlock and it felt like she'd forgotten the combination.

'Do not pass anything to the prisoner! Remember?'

'Yes, now I remember!' I said, in a voice like a wounded seagull. 'But this is a present for my old mucky mucker Moll! Can't I hand it to her?'

'No!'

'What can I do?'

'You could waft it, I suppose.'

And so Long John, Ho and I began flapping our caps over the opening of the bag and urged the air towards Molly. She inhaled deeply.

'Ah!' she said. 'I miss smells like that!'

Suddenly she leapt to her feet and bounded over to the bars.

'I've just remembered I've got something to tell you.' She winked at me. 'It's a secret!'

I sighed. I ordered Long John and Ho to put their fingers in each other's ears and Spot flew under my hat.

I placed my own ears closer to the bars and Moll leaned forward.

'I know who the Scarlet Winkle is!' she giggled gleefully, and she slapped her knees.

'Who?' I hissed.

'You'll never guess!'

'Who?'

'I was chatting to the Old Spice Girls at lunch and they told me that . . .'

'Who?' I bellowed.

'They said the Scarlet Winkle was an alias used by . . .'

Suddenly, an alarm bell erupted in the room and its piercing ding washed out Molly's words like writing in the sand. I tried to get her to repeat herself but 'twas no use.

'What did you say?' I shouted as the dinging died.

'I said visiting time's over!' But this voice belonged to Officer Stump, who grabbed my neckerchief and towed me through the clanging door and on to the streets of Washed-upon-the-Beach.

'Crabs and limpets!' I swore as we arrived on the street.

Spot fluttered out from under my hat.

'Did you hear what she said?' I asked my birdy cohort.

Spot shook his head, pleased he'd done his duty.

'Next time, listen when I tell you not to – you missed a vital clue!'

Spot tutted and hopped on to my shoulder.

Long John and Ho still had their fingers in each other's ears. I let them stay that way and enjoyed a quiet walk home.

I remembered the promise I had made Molly and on my return to the Naughty Lass decided to engage the services of Joe 'Greasy' Spoon. He was the finest solicitor ever to enter a courtroom and an old bilge-room buddy of mine.

Before I could set this plan in motion, however, another obstacle hove into view. As we stomped homeward from the prison a small boy leapt out in front of us, brandishing a rolled-up newspaper. He struck a pose like a grand pirate and I instinctively felt for my trusty old sword, but I soon discovered I no longer owned one.

Before I could put one of my clever plans into operation, Long John leapt forward and thrust himself betwixt the crew and the paperboy.

'What is it you want, you loathsome landlubber?'

The boy twirled his paper threateningly.

'*Daily Splash*! Read all about it!'

He started to circle us, his eyes never leaving his prey.

'All the latest seafaring news! All the tip-top sports stories and, of course, your guide to all that's best on TV!'

'Twas an odd way to sell papers, I thought.

'And how much will you be a-wanting for this rag?' inquired Long John, slipping his hand into his pocket.

'A bargain at ten pounds!'

Long John scoffed and shot a sneering look at the young lad, who quaked not a jot.

'Too much!' said Long John, slowly and calmly.

'Then maybe I can cut you a deal. Let no one say Inky Keith won't see reason! Do you like sport?'

'No!' I said, from behind Long John.

With one swift move, Inky Keith tore the sports section from the paper.

'There – no sport pages – eight pounds.'

Long John scoffed once more.

'Eight pounds? You jest!'

'Do you read your horoscopes?'

''Tis hogwash!' I said, getting the hang of this.

He tore the horoscopes from the paper and declared, 'Seven pounds fifty!'

We slowly negotiated the paper down to just the news section, though I had to argue with Ho over the cookery pages.

'There!' said Inky Keith, holding two battered pages. 'That'll be one pound fifty.'

And with that Long John took his hand from his pocket, but it wasn't coins he was producing. Oh, no. Two peanuts found their way into his mouth. He held back his head and, with two whip-cracking gobs, dispatched them at Inky Keith.

'My ears, my ears! I can't feel my ears!'

The boy fell in a heap on his bag of papers. Long John snatched our two pages from the floor and we scuttled merrily away.

And as we scuttled I noticed the price on the front of the *Daily Splash* – twenty pence. Heigh-ho.

I sat in the living room of the Naughty Lass with a foaming mug of grog in my grasp and pondered the voyage so far. Here I was with the most confuddling case I'd had in years and half my crew were slammed up. I comforted myself with the thought that we'd soon spring Molly and we'd have a full complement once again – ready to solve the mystery of the kidnapped lighthouse. Molly was as innocent as an iceberg and I would prove it.

I flicked open the two pages of the *Daily Splash* and what I saw nearly made me fall off my chair. A gasp popped out of my mouth. I couldn't believe my naval eyes as I gazed at the front page.

TELL-TALE TOOTH MARKS
FOUND ALL OVER TOWN

I ran my beady eye down the column. It seemed that tooth marks had been appearing in homes all over Washed-upon-the-Beach. And the article concluded by suggesting that our very own Molly Meakins was the culprit.

I scrunched the paper into a ball and tossed it over my shoulder. Spot swooped from his perch and head-butted the ball. It landed in the waste bin.

'Twas a desperate time and desperate times call for desperate measures. I slurped a desperate measure of grog and called for Ho.

'What now?' he asked.

'Draw closer, pal!' I whispered, beckoning him nearer.

'Why are you whispering?' he asked. 'I'm not deaf.'

He came over to the wonky coffee table and joined Spot and me in a huddle.

'Dark thoughts are emerging from my watery mind, Ho! The next stretch of our voyage is to be kept among us two . . .'

Spot squawked indignantly.

'Us three, then!'

Spot nodded.

I threw my arms around the shoulders of my piratical pals and drew them closer still.

'I don't want other folk to hear! Especially that gobby swabbie upstairs.' I pointed upwards and we could hear the merry splashing of Long John taking his annual bath. 'If you know what I mean. I have decided we need help. We're going to visit Bootleg Bess.'

'Not Bootleg Bess!' repeated Ho in a shivering voice.

'Yes,' I said, thumbing the last bit of froth into my mouth. 'Bootleg Bess.'

Now you're probably a-wondering who Bootleg Bess was and why she struck fear into the heart of a hardy tar like Ho. Bootleg Bess and I went back many years. She was the sneakiest quarter-mistress ever to helm a schooner. She was known throughout the pirating world as the woman who could get anything anywhere for anyone. Pearls from Morocco, gold from Abyssinia, llamas from Peru, whelks from Clacton – all, of course, for a hefty price. She was the mistress-mind behind the illegal import of 2,000 tons of rice from China – the famous adventure of the ill-gotten grains.

Like most pirates from the old days, she'd hung up her anchor, but unlike others she'd opened a small souvenir shop down by the beach. However, her naughty nautical ways hadn't ceased. Far from it. Her shop was famed throughout the underwater underworld as a front for many illegal doings. A front on the front, as it were.

Rarely would I bandy words with her these days, but I needed information and, more importantly, I needed something very special which only she could provide.

These thoughts eddied through my mind. And so Ho, Spot and I quietly slipped our mooring from the Naughty Lass and set a course for Bootleg Bess's Emporium of Naval Fluff.

The bell tinkled as we opened the door. The musty and dank shop was a-stuffed with all manner of maritime memorabilia, such as Captain Bligh's hula-hoop and a Sink-me-Quick hat with a picture of the *Titanic* on it. Ho was amusing himself with the Marie Celeste Candy Floss machine, while Spot was toying with the selection of Admiral Nelson's eyepatches – one for every sea battle.

'Sam Hawkins!' growled a voice from the depths of my past. It sounded like an anchor scraping on coral.

Bootleg Bess emerged from the darkness at the rear of the shop. She'd not changed a bit. Tall and lank, with skin like a palm tree, she stood before me. Her poky eyes peered out from under two slices of eyebrows. And she still had her leather ear. She lost her own while chasing the sinister Chinese pirate Dip Toh up the rigging of the *Giddy Kipper* after he'd snaffled a stash of valuable shellfish from under her very treasure chest. 'Twas the time of the Teacup Storms and, as Dip clambered up the rigging, a clack of lightning struck the bag, scattering its contents. One surprisingly sharp oyster fell deckwards and sliced Bess's ear clean off. Today, for reasons of vanity, she wears a leather replacement. Despite the fact she powders it every morning, it is none too convincing.

'I see Molly Meakins has finally got her just deserts! The lumpy mermaid!'

She knew about it already. She may have only one ear, but she keeps it close to the ground. I reared up and was about to counter her insult with a well-aimed salvo of words, but then I remembered we needed her help, so I reared back down again.

Ho jumped in.

'Molly is a very good girl. She doesn't do any pirating or buccaneering any more. Unlike some people!'

I wish Ho wouldn't stick his oar in so often. This was a delicate negotiation and I didn't want him wrecking it.

'What a pretty young guppy. Where did you net this one, Hawkins?'

I smiled and twiddled my neckerchief.

'I rescued him single-handed from the dangerous waters of Kowloon Bay.'

Ho strode over to Bess.

'And if he'd left me in a little longer I might have been rescued by someone with money.'

Spot fluttered over and landed on the counter. Bess patted his head.

'And old Spot – 'tis a long time since we were nose to beak.' She slowly stroked Spot's wing with her spindly fingers.

'What do you want, Hawkins?'

She lit a thin cigar and smoke twirled through the air.

I leaned against the counter and tried to look casual.

'I need some information . . .'

'I can give you any information you want – for a price. For example, slip me a single pound coin and I could tell you something that will be of immediate use to you.'

I tore a coin from my pocket and eagerly slid it across the counter. I quickly remembered my image and once more tried to look casual. I placed my elbows on the counter.

'What vital information can you impart?'

'Well, for a pound I could tell you you've just put your elbow in my ashtray!'

I snatched my elbow off the counter and patted the stinky remnants from my jacket as Bess pocketed the pound.

Ho and Spot giggled alongside Bess, but soon we were back on course.

'I need to know the true identity of the Scarlet Winkle. Have you heard of him?'

Bess exhaled vile smoke into the air and it formed shafts in what little sunlight broke into the shop.

'I might have. His true identity is cloaked in mystery. I could find out for you. However, it'll cost.'

'How much?' said Ho excitedly.

I placed my hand on Ho's shoulder.

'Excuse me, who's the captain of this crew?' I asked.

'You are!' He shrugged and stepped back.

I adjusted my hat and spoke.

'How much?'

'Five hundred pounds!' she said.

I was aghast. I knew I hadn't been part of the piratical world for some time, but prices had certainly soared.

Ho giggled and said, 'Maybe I should have asked after all!'

I stood aside and pushed him forward.

'Go on, then, Ho!' I said.

He eyed Bootleg Bess up and down and asked, 'How much?'

'Five hundred pounds!' she repeated.

I drummed my fingers on the counter and contemplated my next move. Spot drummed his claws in support.

'Very well. When you bring me the information, I shall give you the cash.'

'Deal!' she said.

I leaned a little closer.

'And one other thing I need . . .'

'Yes?'

Her cold eyes met mine and a shiver ran up and down my back, across my shoulders, down my arm and out of my thumb. Spot shivered in surprise.

'What do you need?'

I took a deep breath, then said softly, 'I need a submarine!'

Chapter Seven

Idecided 'twas high time to put my nautical noodle to work! I needed to do some serious thinking about this case, which had so far confuddled, bemuddled and bemused me. I took my coat from the hat-stand and wandered out into the dazzling sunlight of Washed-upon-the-Beach.

I strolled along the streets and before long found myself a-walking along the towpath of Clackitt's Canal. 'Twas a manky old place, but once Sid Clackitt's proud barges plied back and forth along its waters, delivering clams to the north and cockles to the south. Running parallel to Clackitt's Canal were the tracks of the Great White Rail Company – also unused for years. 'Twas called the Great White Rail Company because its engines were dressed in the finest white livery and polished brightly every day.

I dragged my drifting thoughts back to the case in hand.

Who would steal a lighthouse?

Suspects: one – Harvey Clump of Clump International Promotions. He would want the lighthouse removed to make way for his rock stadium. When I cleverly questioned him, though, he claimed he wanted to *keep* the lighthouse as the central attraction at the festival. He even showed me the plans. What better way to cover his tracks? I nibbled my nails as I considered this and wandered.

And what of the ransom note that led to the arrest of poor old Moll? How had Molly's tooth marks got on to the piece of paper? If Moll was being framed, why? This case was proving itself a darker and more mysterious mystery than any I'd ever encountered. So many questions and so few answers, yet 'twas answers I sought. I couldn't leave merry Moll lying in that mouldy hold for much longer. We'd weathered too many storms together and I was determined to spring her.

And who was the Scarlet Winkle? We'd soon dredge up his identity – Bootleg Bess was on that particular case and would soon come up trumps. I hoped.

In the distance I heard a siren blow. Not a factory-like siren, no, no. This was a steam siren used on tramp steamers or showboats, but why would a tramp streamer be so far inland?

I turned and suddenly my seagull eye saw a stunning sight. Exploding from the tunnel, like a cork from an old grog bottle, was a fine steam engine from the Great White Rail Company. It came thundering towards me at a rare rate of knots, screaming as it went. I saluted proudly as it screamed past me, blasting my hair and blowing off my hat. The entire train was painted in traditional white. 'Twas a stunning, beautiful and inspiring sight. And down the side was emblazoned its name: 'The Chuffing Shunter'.

On arriving back in Puddle Lane, my eye fell on a less awesome sight. I would have liked to be able to say both my eyes fell on this sight but, as a cashew nut had hit me in one eye, it was down to the other to do the falling. I hastily extracted the nut and wondered from where it had come. I didn't need to wonder long.

There in the little garden in front of the Naughty Lass were Ho and Long John. Tottering on the hedge was an old bilge bucket they were using for target practice. Long John was initiating Ho into the strange

world of spitting. Ho, with a child's bib around his little neck, was eager to learn.

'No, no, no!' explained Long John, slapping his
forehead in exasperation. 'Crane back your neck,
then, just as the nut leaves your lips, snap your head
forward, giving it that extra bit of projection!'

I watched as Ho tried again. He inserted a nut,
pulled back his head and spat. The nut leapt from his
lips, tumbled down his bib and plopped into the fish
pond.

I bounced through the gate and up to my mucky
muckers.

'Heave-ho!' I bellowed heartily.

Ho inserted another nut as I arrived. I didn't notice
this, but if I had, I wouldn't have slapped him on the
back so heartily.

'Old Sam has a plan!' I bellowed again, and slapped
Long John, who didn't look like he enjoyed being
slapped. But you can't take a slap back, can you?

Ho coughed slightly.

''Tis my plan to go looking for evidence of the
whereabouts of the lost lighthouse, my maritime
maties. 'Tis time to grasp this sloop of a mystery by the
tiller and pilot a course for home . . .'

Ho coughed again, a little more loudly.

'I been a-thinking and a-dwelling a little too long,
pals. 'Tis time for action.'

Ho coughed even more.

'Ho, if you want to make a noise, do it quietly!'

He was looking confused and started pointing at his throat.

Long John shifted his attention towards Ho.

'Yes, indeedy, to solve this crime we must . . .'

Ho was wheezing and turning an odd colour. Suddenly, Long John leapt behind him, clasped his arms around Ho's skinny hull and, with one swift move, tugged a folded fist into his sternum.

For a second Ho looked as if he'd got a shoal of angry crabs in his pants. Then suddenly a cashew nut was launched from his mouth, followed by a capful of dribble. With a sigh of relief, we watched it fly through the air, curl in mid-flight and land with a resounding 'ding' in the bilge bucket.

From the upstairs window Spot applauded merrily and made a mark on the score chart.

'It was a good shot!' mused Long John as we tramped along the path towards the cliffs.

'Good shot!' echoed Spot as he fluttered behind.

'Good shot!' repeated Ho merrily as he skipped alongside.

'That's enough spitting for one day,' I ordered. 'We have a case to solve. That is why, my salty mates, we are making our way to the place where the lighthouse was last seen. And do you want to know why?'

No answer came.

I stopped mid-tramp and put my hands on my hips. 'Do you want to know *why*?'

The others stopped and exchanged a look.

'Why, Sam?' they chorused, and we all started off again as I answered.

'Because my old seafaring eyes might have missed something last time I was here. And I might miss something again this time,' I said, pointing at my nutted eye.

'Sorry, boss,' said Ho.

'That's why I need two extra pairs of—'

Spot squawked loudly and pointed at his own little black eyes.

'Three extra pairs.'

And with that we found ourselves on top of the cliff.

Construction work had already begun on the stadium and little diggers and tractors shot back and forth around the remnants of the Pointy Head Lighthouse.

'Now, let us remember, we are detectives here to uncover clues that remain unnoticed by the naked eye—'

'Boss!' Ho tugged at my tunic.

I ignored him.

'We need to keep our eyes to the grindstone—'

'Boss!!'

'Our ears to the pulse—'

'Boss!!'

'And our fingers to the ground!'

Ho tugged at my tunic frantically.

'And if we fail in our mission, let the ground open up and . . .'

At that point the ground opened up and swallowed me.

ARRRGGHHHHHHHHH!

I crashed downwards. Bang, crash, dollop! Bang, crash, dollop!

Finally I landed in a groaning heap, grazed and slightly bruised.

All around was black. A twinkle of light beamed from a hole above. Two heads appeared, silhouetted against the sunlight.

'What the blithering of blue blazes has happened?' I bellowed upwards.

The hole above seemed a long way away. It was.

'Anything broken, boss?' said Ho's voice in the distance.

'No!' I said, looking around. 'There's nothing down

here to break. But where am I?'

Long John bellowed an answer.

''Tis a hole in the ground, Sam, a big, black hole in the ground.'

I'd figured that out for myself.

'Go and fetch help. And send down Spot with some supplies.'

If I was going to be down here for a while, I might as well make myself comfy.

Before long I was sitting on a rock deep, deep in the ground, with a can of grog in my hand and a parrot on my shoulder.

Spot was bandaging my slightly bonked head as I pondered my situation.

'Won't be long before we're free, Spot. And then back behind the wheel of this mystery, eh? Anyway, while we're here we can look for clues.'

Spot sighed. Then I heard the scratching.

'Are you scratching, Spot?'

Spot shook his head and fluttered over to the side of the hole. 'Twas a little dark to see, but being a resourceful parrot he had brought some candles down among the supplies. I lit one.

The hole was dark and grimy. Soil and dirt were all about.

The scratching occurred again.

Spot nodded at the side of the hole. He hovered by

the muddy wall and gestured towards it frantically. He placed his claws on the wall and started to scrape away at some of the soil. Suddenly something strange happened. Something that made the parrot squawk and the pirate quake. Poking out of the soily wall was a small, silver teaspoon. I rubbed my good eye. Yes, 'twas a teaspoon. I held up the candle and peered closer. Shadows danced all around the hole as something even stranger emerged. Holding on to the teaspoon was a hand – a human hand.

Spot and I exchanged a frightened glance and we both gulped the quietest gulps we dared.

Suddenly, there was a huge crunching sound, followed by a massive deluge of soil and muck. We coughed and spluttered and tried to waft away the filth. The cloud of dust blew out my candle and I hastily scrabbled to find a match to relight it.

The dust was settling as the hole was once more suffused with candle glow. Spot and I looked about. Our eyes slowly became used to the half-light once more. And as we became used to the light, we became used to the fact we had visitors.

'Hello, we're the Old Spice Girls. Isn't this super?'

Before us stood two ladies of an uncertain age, though I was certain they were the wrong side of sixty. Both had their grey hair in plaits and each clutched a torch in one hand and a teaspoon in the other. I was unsure of the correct etiquette for meeting strangers in a hole in the ground, so I simply doffed my hat.

'Sam Hawkins, Pirate Detective, and this is my parrot, Spot.'

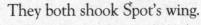

They both shook Spot's wing.

'What a coincidence. Isn't this a coincidence, Gert.'

'It certainly is, Daisy!'

A ship's bell was dinging wildly at the back of my mind.

'Wow, is that Grog-Max? My favourite.'

Gert snatched my can and slurped it gratefully, then handed it to Daisy, who emptied it swiftly. She handed the empty can to Spot.

'Super! We haven't slurped Grog-Max for a very long time.'

I tried to gather my thoughts and ask some leading questions. What was it they had said? Old Spice Girls? I'd heard someone mention them recently.

'Coincidence? Why is this a coincidence?' I asked.

'Because we know a friend of yours.' Gert winked at me.

'Who?'

'Who?' echoed Spot.

'Molly Meakins!' said Daisy.

The distant bell stopped dinging.

'We went to the same prison together!'

Daisy waggled her spoon gleefully before my bewildered eyes. 'But we've managed to escape. Isn't it all so jolly!'

Gert put her arm about my shoulder and continued the story.

'You see, I'd put a poster up of my favourite film star, Dom Cruise. Now, the plaster behind the poster was a little weak and at night I picked away at it. Then we realized the plaster was so weak we could dig a hole through it and so we did – with these!'

They waggled their teaspoons.

'Not the best silver, but it jolly well did the job!'

'And we dug, dug, dug until we found ourselves here – isn't it super? But look at us hogging the whole conversation. Tell us a little about yourself.'

I straightened my neckerchief and wondered what to say.

'I'm on the case of the kidnapped lighthouse,' I said proudly.

The Old Spice Girls sat on a rock as I spoke.

'Now we've heard all about that.'

From above I heard rumbling.

The Old Spice Girls threw themselves to the side of the hole.

'Don't let anyone see us!' they yelled. 'Spoil the fun and all!'

A shadowy head appeared at the hole.

 94

'Boss, we've got help. The construction workers are going to lower a basket down. All you have to do is climb in and we'll pull you to safety!'

'Hoist away, my old pal!' I shouted heartily.

A juddering noise came from above, along with a small basket. Before long the basket was at the base of the hole and I was clambering in it.

I held out my hand to the Old Spice Girls.

'Why don't you come with me?'

Gert giggled.

'Don't be silly. We want our freedom.'

They waggled their teaspoons in unison.

At this point a distant thought came sloshing over the horizon of my memory. It swam like a sea lion towards home, splashed through the shallows and waddled up the beach.

'Wait a minute. Molly told me *you* know the true identity of the Scarlet Winkle!'

'We do!'

'Who is it?'

From above I heard the words, 'Hoist away!'

'The Scarlet Winkle is—'

Their words were suddenly drowned by the juddering sounds of whatever confuddling contraption Ho and Long John had enlisted to drag me out of this hole.

'What did you say?' I shouted.

Gert and Daisy mouthed some more, but the noise was getting louder as I was being pulled further away from them. I tried to read their lips but 'twas no use.

Within seconds I was safely back on the ground, looking at the delighted faces of Ho and Long John and the construction worker who was helping them.

I clambered from the basket.

'Pleased to be back, boss?'

'I should flog the pair of you!' I bellowed, pointing a threatening finger at them both.

The construction worker removed his hard hat and wiped his brow.

'You wouldn't get much for them!'

I stomped away from the construction site and back to the Naughty Lass.

Spot fluttered on behind.

Chapter Eight

I sat in a miffed huff in the Naughty Lass with a steaming mug of grog in my hand and my teeth grinding in my mouth. I was livid!

'What a pair of wet-headed, waddle-brained loons!' I slurped noisily at my grog. 'I wouldn't trust them to navigate their way around a paddling pool!'

In the kitchen there was giggling and banging coming from Long John and Ho, but I took no notice. Those two goons could have single-handedly scuppered this entire voyage. And it was meant to be my return to glory!

Suddenly, the door squealed on its hinges and in they burst. Both were wrapped in sheets snaffled from the airing cupboard and both were grasping large white hankies. My large white hankies, in fact.

Long John was making an announcement as if I was a large audience. I sighed inwardly and outwardly, at the same time.

'And now, ladies and gentlemen, a little tune to charm you from your grumpy depths. An old nose-blowing favourite from yesteryear, "Snot Unusual"!'

And with that Ho and Long John embarked on a strange and enthusiastic rendition of the old Tom Bones hit shanty. They were not singing, you understand, they were blowing their noses in rhythm and almost in tune. 'Twas a brave effort to cheer up their boss, but I was not to be won over so easily.

I leapt up and yanked the hankies from their noses.

'Boss!' pleaded Ho. 'We're trying to cheer you up by doing some nose blowing. You told me you used to enjoy it when you were young! You said the Cockle Triplets used to blow their noses for you all the time.'

'Yes, but their noses were a lot prettier than yours! Sit down!'

Long John and Ho sat down, looking like two guilty pilchards.

'There it was!' I slammed the mug on the wonky coffee table and startled the parrot. 'Right in the palm of my hand!' I showed my palm to emphasize the point.

'It's empty, boss,' said Ho quietly.

'Of course it's empty, you dribbling drip!'

I jumped up and stomped about the living room. I always stomp when I'm annoyed, and I was very annoyed, so did a lot of stomping.

'Do you realize the solution to this mighty mystery was in the palm of my hand? I was about to find out the true identity of the Scarlet Winkle.' I whirled around and stared at them. 'And what did you do?'

'What did you do?' repeated the parrot.

Long John and Ho looked at each and said in unison, 'We rescued you.'

'Yes, you burbling lumps of seaweed, you rescued me. From now on – never, ever rescue me again!'

'OK, boss, if you say so.' And Ho crossed his legs and shifted his attention to a cookery book.

I stomped from the room, slamming the door behind me.

I had to come back a few minutes later to fetch my hat.

I was sitting on the creaky, squeaky rocking chair in my bedroom, idly making shadow puppets in the light from the lamp that hung by my hammock. I tried to make the shape Billy Buddy had made the day he revealed he was the hands behind the Rockness Monster. But 'twas not an easy thing to do. I wiggled my thumbs, but the shadow just looked like two tubby fists. These nautical hands had tied some of the most complex knots known to man, I thought, but could they make a little shadow monster?

There was a knock on the door.

'What?' I shouted, starting to untangle my fingers.

Ho poked his little face round the corner and entered the room like a worried porpoise swimming near a grumpy shark.

'Boss, I just came to say . . .' His gaze was caught by my handy silhouette. 'What you doing, boss?'

'Trying to make a Rockness Monster!'

Ho looked a little confused. I explained.

'If we don't find the Pointy Head Lighthouse, we'll never see the Rockness Monster again.'

Ho looked even more confused. I explained again.

'Billy Buddy does the Rockness Monster, you see. It's a shadow puppet.' I waggled my thumbs to demonstrate. 'He holds his hands in the beam of Bessie the Bulb and a huge shadow appears.'

'Wow! Billy Buddy is the Rockness Monster. That's brilliant! But doing shadow puppets is dead easy. Look – a bunny!'

Ho waggled his little fingers in the light and, as if by magic, a rabbit appeared on my wall.

'How did you do that?' I said, grabbing his little hands and inspecting them.

Ho winked and tapped his nose. I tapped mine, but it didn't make any difference.

I switched off the lamp.

'Anyway, what do you want?'

'Telephone call, boss,' he said softly, pulling our portable phone from his pocket and holding it out for me.

I placed the handset to my shell-like. 'Sam Hawkins, award-winning Pirate Detective, speaking.'

'Twas Bootleg Bess herself. Seems she had managed to get her cold hands on a submarine. She might be a slimy creature used to swimming in deep waters, but she could dredge up any supplies when offered hard cash. All I had to do was find some hard cash.

'Ho!' I cried. 'Fetch your piggy bank!'

'Twas another bright and beautiful day in old Washed-upon-the-Beach. I might have pillaged and plundered my way across the globe, but this was home.

The wind was once more in my hair as we putt-putted on the Nippy Clipper along the coast to meet Bootleg Bess at the bottom of the cliffs. I had dark suspicions about Long John Saliva. Why, for example, was a talented pirate so short of cash? And wasn't it odd that he arrived at the Naughty Lass at the same time as the ransom note? I would need to keep my seagull eye on him, so I brought him along too. And what voyage would be complete without Ho and Spot – fine

companions who'd trust me with their lives. They hugged their old boss as we screeched around another corner.

Before long the beach came into view, and so did Bootleg Bess. She was standing there on her own, surrounded by what looked like some rusty old barrels, but I couldn't see any submarine. What cunning plot was coursing through her dark mind?

I dismounted as we arrived at the beach and scurried over to the querky quarter-mistress.

'What blithering high jinks are you about, Bess? You said you had a submarine for me. I have the cash!'

I held up Ho's piggy bank.

'And I have the submarine!' She gestured behind her at the pile of barrels. 'Sam Hawkins, this is *The Plunging Duck*. One of the oldest and most trusted submarines ever to scrape the bottom of the ocean. In this very submersible Three-nostrils MacTavish sank HMS *Shipshape*.' She circled the barrels hypnotically. My eyes began to swim. ''Twas in this very vessel No-buttocks Finchley rescued a sack of Oriental oysters from certain death. This vessel has been skippered by the greatest naval folk in history.' She slid over to me and whispered in my ear. 'Except one.'

'Me!' I said, in a voice filled with wonder.

I barely noticed her slip the piggy bank from my grasp.

'Then 'tis time for *The Plunging Duck* to meet the

greatest of them all! Now listen carefully . . .'

I gazed down at *The Plunging Duck* as her words washed over me. To be up there with No-buttocks and Three-nostrils made my heart beat with excitement. The vessel was beautifully set out and crafted by the finest boat builders ever to chip oak. The varnished wooden hold was bedecked with opulent velvet upholstery. Ah, to get my clammy hands on this beauty!

'. . . otherwise you'll be blown out of the water,' she finished as I nodded glazy-eyed at the vessel.

'All aboard!' I shouted, flinging open the porthole, and leapt inside.

The porthole door was slammed shut behind me. Through the tiny and mucky window I could glimpse Long John and Ho and Bootleg Bess as they started to push *The Plunging Duck* seawards.

But why, you may be a-thinking, do I need a submarine? Well, my maritime mind had been a-pondering the problems set before me. To steal a lighthouse was not an easy task and to hide one was even harder. There were clearly no clues at the site where the Pointy Head Lighthouse had once stood. And there were no clues below the lighthouse, as I'd discovered when I was stranded in that hole with the Old Spice Girls. So if the lighthouse hadn't gone down, I thought, it might have gone out to sea, see? All I needed was to bob along the bottom of the briny for a while and try to track down some clues.

'Simple!' I said to myself.

'Simple!' echoed Spot.

Squid oil! What was he doing here?

'What are you doing here?' I asked.

Spot nodded towards the porthole. He must have squeezed in just as the door was being sealed.

'There's not enough oxygen for two!' I sighed, but then he only had little lungs. 'Right, you can stay, but keep your eyes peeled!'

With that Spot shot to the window and we both watched in awe as we plunged below the waves.

Now, I'd like to say what a stunning and beautiful experience it was. I'd like to tell you about the colourful fish and the amazing coral reefs. But this was Washed-upon-the-Beach after all.

We passed a Kwik-Wave Supermarket trolley and an old bike frame and a couple of boots. No clues so far.

Spot and I pressed our faces against the cold glass of the porthole and gazed out.

I gritted my teeth and crossed my fingers. So did Spot. Please let there be one tiny clue here, I thought, just one.

And then I saw it. My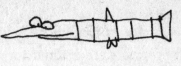
salty eye fell on a sight to
bring joy to the hardiest of
hearts.

'Twas a brick, and not just any old brick. This was a white brick. As white as the Pointy Head Lighthouse. And, my detecting eye spotted, 'twas not covered with mould or mildew. That meant it couldn't have been underwater for very long. Ha! Now to net my catch.

I looked about the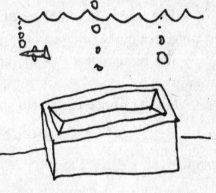
array of knobs and
buttons before me.

Which of these
would operate the
grabbing-arm attach-
ment? It must be one
of them. If only I'd
paid attention. There
was only one way to decide.

'Meany, miny, moany min, catch a guppy by the fin, if it squeals throw it back in, meany, miny, moany min.' I chose the long red lever to my right.

Spot leapt over and grabbed my tunic sleeve in his beak.

'Now, now, Spot. No time for games!' I gave one hearty yank on the lever.

WHOOSH!!!

We were ejected into the air and were rocketing up at too many knots to count. We came to a halt way up high, and then gravity started to do what gravity does. Within the blink of an eye, we had changed direction and found ourselves plummeting towards earth, towards the beach in fact, towards a nice sandcastle Ho had just built.

CRASH! BANG! CRUNCH!

The sandcastle collapsed under the combined weight of pirate and parrot.

We both looked about, groaned and fell into a faint.

I didn't notice Ho placing a flag in my hat.

My brain was pitching and tossing inside my head as I awoke. I was back at the Naughty Lass in my hammock and Ho was applying some strange Oriental ointment to my head. Beside me lay little Spot, looking stunned and confused in my sock drawer. Ho applied the same ointment to him too.

'What happened?' I asked wearily.

'What happened?' Spot echoed the words, but without his usual enthusiasm. Ho gave no answer.

I ambled down into the living room later that evening and all was as still as a haddock on a fishmonger's slab.

Seems I'd been asleep for quite a while. Spot fluttered gingerly into the room and on to my shoulder. He looked about as quizzically as I did.

Where had they all gone?

Spot drew my attention to a note on the wonky coffee table.

I opened it and read:

Get well soon, boss. Me and Long John and Bootleg Bess are all having a night out at the Black Spot Tavern. It's karaoke night!
See you later.
Your old pal,
Ho

Pah! Just when I needed a little bit of company. There I was in my bed of sickness and they had skipped ship. Typical!

I decided to spend some time pondering the case in hand. I idly thought about the lighthouse. Why would anyone steal a lighthouse? How would they steal a lighthouse? Hmm, so much to consider. The case was a pressing one and no time could be wasted. I must plunge on and solve the mystery.

It wasn't long before I was asleep.

Chapter Nine

'Twas a dark, dull and quiet night and I was all a-slumber in my comfy hammock. The moon was beaming merrily over Washed-upon-the-Beach and I was having a slightly unsettling dream about cheese. I tossed and turned and tried to change the subject of my dream, but the nasty stuff kept coming bobbing to the surface.

Tap!

I decided to swap my cheesy dream for one of derring-do on the high seas.

Tap!

What dirty dogfish was interrupting my slumber?

Tap!

I pricked up my detecting ears and attempted to locate the source of the noise.

Tap!

'Twas coming from the window! I wrapped the

duvet around my tubby hull and padded over. As soon as I slid open the window I realized what was a-happening.

Below the window were Ho, Long John and Bootleg Bess nestling together like a shoal of gold-fish, gazing up at me. Long John had been spitting peanuts at the window to attract my attention. Me old pals were back from their night at the Black Spot Tavern!

A voice spoke, but it didn't sound like one of the three.

'Do these belong to you?'

I strained a little further out of the window. Standing by the front door were Officers Stump and Stibbins. Fish bait!

I swiftly eeled into some clothes and rushed down-stairs.

I threw open the door to my visitors.

'Enter!' I said heartily.

Stump had a face like a slapped whelk as she stepped in.

'Why are you spitting peanuts at my window?' I asked as they crowded in behind her.

'Because your doorbell doesn't work!' said Stibbins, helping himself to an apple from the fruit bowl.

'Did you know your doorbell doesn't work?' asked Stump, taking a banana.

'Yes,' I said, "tis the only way I can get any sleep some nights!'

The gang of pirates found seats in the living room and all seemed a tad sheepish.

I soon cottoned on to this and asked Stump, 'Is something amiss, miss?'

'It's ms actually. Yes, there is something amiss. I have just arrested these people for breaking and entering.'

I slumped into the settee and smacked my forehead.

'Ho! I can't believe my ears!'

'But as they failed in their attempt, we decided not to charge them!' She munched her banana. 'It's not often we get people breaking into jail. Usually it's the other way round.'

I leapt to my feet and pumped Stump's hand.

'Officer, I owe you a thousand thanks!'

'Just a couple will do!'

'Thank you, thank you! I'll put the rest in an envelope and send it to the police station.'

And with that the officers were gone, leaving a strong smell of aftershave and some very sour faces.

I made sure that the police were safely out of the way, then I turned the tide.

'What in the bluest of blue brinies has happened, you squid-headed bunch of blowfish! I'm a pirate of

standing in this community. You can't go around getting arrested. What happened?'

Bootleg Bess and Long John both pointed at Ho.

'His idea!' they chorused.

Ho jumped up and started stomping back and forth.

'Yes, actually, it was my idea, actually, and I'm very proud of it. It just went wrong, that's all.'

Ho stomped back and forth, and Spot watched him pace as if he was a packet of birdseed on a string.

I drummed my fingers on the arm of the settee and tried to calm my nautical nerves.

'What . . .'

Drum, drum, drum . . .

'. . . actually . . .'

Drum, drum, drum . . .

'. . . happened?'

I lost my cool and banged the arm of the settee. The parrot jumped and almost disappeared in a cloud of dust.

And so little Ho, whom I had single-handedly saved from death in Kowloon Bay, began his tale.

Seems they were in the Black Spot Tavern, quaffing grog till the early hours of the morn. Seems they had much to celebrate. They'd won the shanty karaoke, apparently, by singing the 'Trout Calypso', a popular ditty with the young folk. I'd never heard of it.

Anyway, the prize was a dozen flagons of grog and a family ticket to Leisure Island. The grog was swilled down and the ticket pocketed.

Seems things got a little wilder thereafter. The night wore on, the singing got louder and Ho tried to teach Bess the Tuna Two-Step, but 'twas when they started juggling fish pies the barman began to object.

And so they found themselves in a sprawling heap on the steps of the tavern. At this point any self-respecting buccaneer would have high-tailed it back to port and hidden his head under his pillow. But not Ho. Oh, no!

Ho, clever Ho, bright and intelligent Ho, who was taught everything he knows by the finest pirate to catch a cannonball, decided on a different course of action. Ho decided they all ought to break into the Washed-upon-the-Beach jail and rescue Molly. And being washed away with the heady excitement of the evening, they all agreed.

No tools did they have, but they still pressed on with an exploit that would bring shame upon the Naughty Lass. They scuttled towards the jail, keeping in the shadows all the way. Ho had a plan and he shared it with his conspirators.

The jail wall had atop it an electric beam which, when broken, sets off an alarm. Ho enlisted Long John's spitting talents to *deliberately* set off the alarm.

113

Why deliberately? Well, old Ho was a cunning little shrimp. He figured that if he set off the alarm a number of times in succession the guards would tumble from their den and have a sniff about, but would find nothing. And if the alarm kept going off, they would eventually assume it was faulty and no longer respond. It worked.

After the tenth alarm the guards stopped coming. This was Ho's cue to climb the wall. And climb he did. And clamber and scrape. Leaving the others on the other side of the wall (after all, they needed someone to catch Molly when they returned). He prised open a window and crept into the jail.

Ho was quiet as a sea-slug as he made his way through the darkened corridors of the jail. 'Twas a brave and hearty thing to do. In that jail resided some of the filthiest criminals ever to slither across the world of crime. Ho was taking great risks to rescue his pal.

He stopped by Moll's door and tapped gently on the metal flap. He slowly opened it and peered in. Peering back was a fierce face like a rusty trawler within a hairnet.

'May I help you?' it hissed.

'I've come to rescue you!'

'I don't want to be rescued – I'm quite comfy here, thank you!' And the flap was snatched from Ho and

114

slammed shut.

Ho opened it again.

'Moll, is that you?'

'No, she got moved out yesterday. Try cell 37!' snarled the voice.

At cell 37 Ho flapped open the flap and peered in. There stood Moll, wearing nothing but a bedsheet. It must have been a hideous sight.

'Where've you been?' she whispered. 'I've been waiting to be rescued every night since I got here!'

'I need a hairgrip to pick this lock!' Ho responded.

'Hold on!' Molly rummaged about in her cell.

While she rummaged, Ho suddenly felt something sticking in his back. The something prodded him and he gave a little yelp. His fingers went to investigate the something and they discovered it was something cold and solid. It was prodding him again. He slowly turned, ran his fingers along it. On the end of it he found a short, blunt and disgruntled police officer.

'Get off my truncheon!' ordered Officer Stump. Seems she had been called by the guards as soon as they discovered their alarm was faulty.

Molly, however, didn't know the police had arrived and poked something through the flap.

'I couldn't find a hairgrip!' she whispered. 'Will an Alice band do?'

As soon as the words left her lips her eyes fell on

Officer Stump.

'Fish sticks!' She looked down at Ho. 'Never seen him before in my life!' she cried, and slammed the flap shut.

Officer Stump clasped Ho in cuffs. The rest of the conspirators had been discovered hiding in a wheelie bin by Officer Stibbins and they were all marched back to the Naughty Lass.

'Twas then they discovered my doorbell didn't work.

I looked at my old pal's grumpy face.

'My only Chinese sea cook arrested! Have I taught you nothing?'

Ho picked up a magazine and turned to the cookery pages.

'You taught me how to pick a lock, boss!'

I mumbled a clever response, I can't remember what it was, and went back to bed.

I sat in my creaky, squeaky armchair in my bedroom and watched the sun rise over Washed-upon-the-Beach. In the distance the birds were a-singing to welcome the day and I wondered how I was going to solve this mystery. I decided 'twas time to put quill to paper and make some notes.

Stolen: Pointy Head Lighthouse, from owner,

> Billy Buddy.
> Clues: one brick lost at sea and a ransom note
>   signed by the Scarlet Winkle.
> Suspects: nil.

'Twas a short list. Even making the writing bigger didn't fill up the page. Curses and cuttlefish! I was paddling in the shallows with only two clues to rub together.

My thoughts were shattered by the shrill bleeping of the phone. I scrabbled about the room and found it in my pants drawer.

'Sam Hawkins, Pirate Detective, speaking!' I said, saluting the phone.

On the other end was a voice I recognized but hadn't heard for a long time.

'You no-good dingbat! You stupid, no-hope dope of a pirate!'

'Twas Lola Schwartz, Mayor of Washed-upon-the-Beach and a dear old pal of mine.

'Lola – how lovely to have your delightful voice in my ear!'

'Cut the carp! I wanna know where the lighthouse is!'

I tangled my finger in my neckerchief.

'Well, 'tis proving a tiresome teaser, your mayorship, I—'

'If you don't get the lighthouse back, Harvey Clump is going to withdraw all his funding for the Rockness Monster Rock Festival. Do you know how much money that brings to Washed-upon-the-Beach each year? Find that Pointy Head Lighthouse or you'll spend the rest of your days fishing leaves from the council paddling pool!'

'Well, all in good time, your parsnip. I—'

But my words were lost in the buzz of the dialling tone. She'd put the phone down on me. Pah! She was a spirited wench, but she'd left me dangling on the end of her line.

I pondered my fate and pulled at my bottom lip.

As I pulled and pondered, a knocking came to the door. This was followed by a ringing. A knocking and a ringing? That rings a bell, I thought, and made for the hallway.

I flung open the doorway and sunlight flooded in. I was about to give a jolly greeting to whoever was there, but nobody was. I looked back and forth. I scuttled down the driveway and looked up and down Puddle Lane, and still nobody was there.

'Pah! Kids . . .' I mumbled as I returned, and then I saw a strange sight. Upon my Welcome Aboard mat was a shiny little object. I bent down and picked it up. 'Twas a brass door knocker.

'Pah! Kids . . .' I mumbled, and went to replace it on my door. But then I got a little confuddled. There was a door knocker already on my door. I couldn't remember having two door knockers, so where had this one come from? I looked up to see if a magpie had shed its load, but none was to be seen. I shrugged and re-entered the Naughty Lass.

I placed the brass door knocker on the wonky coffee table, sat down and started to pull at my bottom lip once more. I didn't pull it for very long.

The phone burst into life again. I snatched it up and held it to my shell-like.

'Lola! Allow me to explain . . .'

But the voice at the end was not Lola's.

'I have a call for you from Mr S. Winkle. Shall I put him through?'

I stared at the telephone. It stared back.

'Yes!' I bellowed down it.

There was a click and then I heard, '*Hawkins! 'Tis I – the Scarlet Winkle!*'

'You yellow-bellied scoundrel – what have you done with the Pointy Head Lighthouse?' I yelled.

'*If you want to see the rest of the lighthouse, then I want gold – and lots of it!*'

'What do you mean the *rest* of the lighthouse?' I asked, fingering the door knocker.

'Did you receive a surprise this morning? Was there a knocker at the door?'

I held the door knocker close to my chest and decided to play for time.

'I'm not sure.'

'Hold the line!'

Then the voice became muffled. He was clearly covering the mouthpiece. But I could make out some screams, a couple of slaps and a strained, pleading little voice. Finally, he came back on the line.

'Did you look on the doormat?' he asked.

'Yes, indeed!' Ha, this is the way to deal with criminals, I thought, then said, 'Where is this knocker from?'

The Scarlet Winkle let out a long, long sigh.

'From the Pointy Head Lighthouse, of course!'

'Where is it?'

'It's in your hand!'

'Not the knocker, the lighthouse!' I shouted, raising my fist to the mouthpiece.

'Do you think I would tell you where it was?'

I pondered his question.

'What if I asked nicely?' I asked nicely and lowered my fist.

'I want lots of gold. There isn't another lighthouse like this for miles around . . .'

And then the first voice entered the conversation.

'This is a premium-rate telephone line and this taunting has so far cost three pounds fifty.'

The Scarlet Winkle snapped back, '*Hush! Fool!*'

'Well, I'm only saying because it is a lot of money!' the voice replied.

'*And I'm about to make a lot more! Remember, Hawkins, gold, gold and more gold.*'

And then the line went dead.

My aquatic brain pondered the thoughts and events. The fiendish felon was right, 'twas the only lighthouse for miles around. Or was it?

'Twas then the anchor plopped, and it plopped with the biggest splash I had yet heard in this case. There is *another* lighthouse. Billy Buddy's little model lighthouse. I gurgled with delight at the thought. Ha! The mist is starting to clear.

I resolved to visit the mad Billy Buddy once more.

Chapter Ten

I stomped into the Red Sea Lion Tavern and rapped on Billy Buddy's door with my finest fist to announce my arrival.

The door opened just a gap and Billy Buddy's eyes peeped out.

'He's in the bath!' said his first voice, and then he slammed the door in my surprised face.

I rapped again, but with a little more urgency.

'Billy, open the door – I have thoughts!'

The door opened once again, but the gap was the same.

'He's clipping his nails!' said his second voice.

I was fleet of foot on this occasion and rammed the aforementioned foot in the gap and, with a well-practised nudge, pressed open the door.

Billy Buddy was sitting on the settee with a towel about his head and a pair of nail clippers in his hand.

'What did you let him in for?' he said.

'*I didn't – you did!*' he replied.

I immediately seized control of the situation.

'Don't worry – either of you. Old Sam is here to help.'

I wandered around the settee and tried to be as casual as possible. I came and sat next to Billy Buddy, humming a little shanty as I did.

'Beautiful day!' I said, gesturing at the outside world.

'Hmmmm,' said Billy, unsure.

'Tell me,' I said, slowly twiddling with my neckerchief in an endearing manner, 'what happened to the lighthouse?'

Billy suddenly shrieked.

'*Stolen! You know it's been stolen! And I wanted you to find it. But up till now you've found absolutely nothing. The lighthouse, our dear old lighthouse, is gone. Gone forever!*'

'No, I mean the model lighthouse you showed me yesterday,' I said.

'Oh, that one's in the suitcase.'

And so Billy Buddy slid the suitcase from under his creaking bed, wiped dusty rust from the locks and sprang it open. He produced the model lighthouse and cradled it in his hands. The sunlight glinted off its tiny windows as it lay there.

'The model Pointy Head Lighthouse!' one of him announced proudly.

'Twas a beautiful model, perfect in every detail. Tiny little doorway, with a tiny little doorstep.

'Could I hold it for minute?' I asked, reaching out my hands.

Billy very gently lowered the model into my waiting grasp. Then I noticed something slightly odd.

'Billy, this is very heavy for a model,' I said, sitting on the settee.

'Hee-heee!' he giggled, placing a hand over his mouth.

'*Hee-heee-heee!*' he giggled, placing a hand over his hand.

'There's something you're not telling me, isn't there, Billy?' I said.

Billy skipped around the settee, giggling as he went and twirling the towel around his head.

'Yes, there is!'

I leapt to my feet, hugged the model to my chest and skipped after him. We did a couple of circuits of the settee – I wasn't entirely sure why – before I said, 'Go on, then, tell me!'

Billy Buddy suddenly stopped and looked about cautiously. He peered under the cushion on the settee and, content there was no one listening, motioned for me to join him in a huddle. He drew the damp towel over both our heads until he was completely satisfied that no one could hear us and then he spoke.

'It's not made out of wood!' he said.

'It's not made out of plastic!' he said.

'It's not made of clay either!' he said.

I was getting restless – like a tug boat bracing itself for a huge tidal wave.

'What is it made from?' I snapped.

'Coins!' he yelled.

'Shh!' he shushed himself, and then whispered the words this time.

'Coins. This model is made from a tower of coins, thirty-five all together.'

He turned the model upside down and showed me the base. 'Twas true as a true thing. The base of the lighthouse was made from a coin and, by the looks of it, 'Twasn't from these shores.

'They're Roman actually! I was told these coins came across with Caesar Salad in 54 BC.'

I gasped. 'Caesar Salad! Wasn't he the one who fiddled with his food as Rome burned?'

'No, that was a different fellow! But apparently Caesar had these coins minted to celebrate his invasion of Britain. He was going to invade up the beaches of Washed-upon-the-Beach and take over the country.'

'What happened?' I asked.

'*The invasion never took place, because his mum said he had to come home for his tea!*'

I gazed at the picture on the coins. A small Caesar grinned back at me.

'*Only thirty-five of those coins were ever made and over the years they have been passed down from lighthouse keeper to lighthouse keeper. Until they fell into our hands.*'

I was still a little confuddled by this.

'But why make them into a lighthouse?'

'Because, Sam, down the years, there have been various attempts to steal the coins by naughty bad people – so we decided to disguise them.'

I nursed the model lighthouse in my hands and mused on this strange discovery.

'And how much do you suppose these coins are worth?' I inquired.

'*No idea!*' came the reply.

'Well, Billy Buddy, I think I know someone who might!'

Dingle-ingle-ing!!!

The shop bell tinkled as we entered Bootleg Bess's

Emporium of Naval Fluff. 'Twas still the mankiest hold on the promenade, but inside was vital information. Or so I hoped. Billy Buddy was by my side, bickering with himself, but I took no notice. If my hunch was right, then this lighthouse could hold valuable clues about my current case. We needed to find the true value of the treasure in our hands.

Bootleg Bess emerged from the darkness at the back of the shop like a conga eel slipping through the porthole of a mouldy shipwreck.

'Sam Hawkins! How nice to see your face again! You've recovered from your voyage aboard *The Plunging Duck* I see!'

'Only just!' I sniffed, massaging my head. 'You ought to give me back my—'

'No refunds!' she screeched, banged the desk bell, and then turned her attention to Billy. 'Oh, look, you've brought a little friend.'

Billy Buddy doffed his hat, then doffed it again.

I had ordered him not to speak, as 'twould only add to the confusion and we needed a straight answer from Bootleg. I explained the history behind this strange model and pointed to the coin at the base of it.

Bootleg was intrigued and held a large magnifying glass to her beady eye.

'Hmm, they're the genuine article all right!' she

said, but then sighed. 'Of course, I don't think they're worth much. Wait . . .'

She drew a book from the shelves behind and her spidery fingers flicked through the pages. She stopped and stabbed at an entry.

'Hmmmm, just as I thought – not worth much. I'll give you five pounds for the lot.' She placed the book to one side, just out of my line of sight.

Billy Buddy was incensed.

'This is my inheritance!'

'*And mine!*'

'It must be worth more than five measily pounds!'

'*At least six!*'

I placed two fingers on his lips, before he could say any more. Bootleg Bess looked at him, suspiciously, like he was something she'd found floating in her soup.

'Perhaps, then, you'd care to make a deal?' I suggested.

Bootleg lit one of her slim cigars and smoke slithered through the air. This mean-spirited maiden was a-tricking us, 'twas clear to me, but what could I do?

'I'm always open to offers!'

I pointed to something on a high shelf. I was hatching a plan.

'Perhaps you'd like to swap it for that stuffed jelly-fish on the shelf!'

She sneered a smile and said, 'Don't be ridiculous.

That jellyfish is worth far more than these coins!'

'Worth more?' I asked.

'Of course,' she replied. 'Have you ever tried to stuff a jellyfish?'

I had to admit I hadn't.

'Very well, Bootleg, I'll swap you this cheap selection of coins for that . . . er . . . . that inflatable skull and crossbones.'

She looked up at the shelf and then back at the coins. An evil little grin scuttled across her face.

'It's a deal!'

Throughout this negotiation, Billy Buddy was frantically digging me in the ribs and making gestures. He wasn't privy to my scam, so all I could do was make gestures back. I gestured him in the eye by mistake.

'Ouch!' he squealed.

Bootleg was getting her stepladder.

'Is something wrong?' she asked.

'No, no, no. Just go and get our prize skull!'

I kept a weather eye on the old trout as she started to mount the ladder. Once her full attention was on the climb, I leaned over the counter and lugged the coin book towards me. 'Twas still open at the page. I read a little and it chilled me.

This was it:

Caesar Salad minted his own coins in metalwork class at Emperer College and made only thirty-five. He intended to issue them once he had conquered Britain. Unfortunately, the conquering was called off early and the coins were lost somewhere in the English Channel. They are the most sought-after coins in the history of monetary matters and are said to be worth £50,000—

I gulped a dry gulp as I read the final word:

each.

Within the blink of a pilchard's eye I had snatched back the little lighthouse, grabbed Billy Buddy's hand and ploughed out of the door.

'Do you want the medium size or extra large?' were the last words I heard as we leapt like salmon through the door.

Dingle-ingle-ing!!!

Back at the Naughty Lass I hastily hurled the little lighthouse into the ship's safe and placed the key on a string about my neck.

Ho, whom I'd grounded for his recent behaviour,

hove into view from the kitchen. He had a wok in one hand and some ice-cream and chives in the other.

'Lunch?' he asked.

Billy Buddy and I started skipping merrily in a circle around him.

'Twas the greatest of all treasure. No single, solitary sailor had ever trawled such bounty. 'Twould go down in history! I leapt about and tweaked Ho's ear playfully.

'Lunch?' he repeated, refusing to acknowledge our joy and jollity.

'Hee-hee, *ho-ho*, hee-hee, *ho-ho*!' Billy Buddy was delighted too – after all, 'twas his treasure.

'All right, all right!' said Ho, banging down his wok. 'What's happened?'

I sat Ho at the table and explained all that had occurred, but I kept the juiciest news till the very end.

'So we went to see Bootleg and, by a very devious and clever plan, I managed to wrestle the truth from her. I've found out the true value of the coins.'

I moved closer to Ho and gleefully announced, 'Each of those thirty-five coins is worth £50,000 – totalling £1,750,000!'

Ho paused.

He looked at Billy Buddy.

He looked at me.

He suddenly shrieked with delight, threw his wok

131

in the air and joined us in a merry dance.

'Twas then we heard the clunk. 'Twas a clunk followed by a groan, followed by a crash, and it came from the other side of the kitchen door.

We halted our capering and I threw open the door. There, sprawled out on the deck, was Long John Saliva, looking like a shocked whale and with a little spit dribbling down his chin. A look of horror was frozen to his face.

The efficient Ho soon brought him to his senses with a small piece of mouldy blue cheese.

He shook his head and looked into my eyes.

'£1,750,000!' he said, gurgled, dribbled and fainted once more.

Chapter Eleven

I left Long John recovering in the Naughty Lass. 'Twas a strange response to the news, I thought, as I walked merrily along the sun-drenched streets of Washed-upon-the-Beach. I pondered what could have caused a well-weathered pirate to capsize like that. Perhaps he was starting to feel a little land-sick after so many years afloat. Heigh-ho! I put a skip in my step as I thought about the coins. Billy Buddy could now afford a generous fee – all we had to do was find his beloved lighthouse.

Lola Schwartz, the beguiling Mayor, had called me on the telephone and asked me to attend a meeting with her. And so off I was going to attend it.

I found the Mayor's office all a-flutter as I sailed into the town hall. 'Twas a thriving hive of activity and for why, you ask? Well, the Rockness Monster Rock Festival was soon to be upon the public. According to the *Daily Splash*, 'twas to be housed in a fine arena the size of twenty galleons. Folks flustered past waving documents, while secretaries scurried to meetings as if their lives depended on it. I slapped a hearty hand on the desk bell, but its dingle was engulfed in noise. I slapped it again. A face emerged from behind a filing cabinet and tentatively approached.

'Can I help?' she said. Her badge read 'Millie'.

'You certainly can, Millie. I have an appointment with Lola Schwartz, the Mayor of Washed-upon-the-Beach!'

'Oh,' she said, unsure what to do next.

I stood there, waiting for her to recognize me.

'And what name is it?'

I stood sideways so she could recognize me from my publicity photos. She thought I was offering her my ear and moved closer to it.

'What . . . name . . . is . . . it?' she repeated slowly.

With a flourish, I answered, 'Sam Hawkins, award-winning Pirate Detective!' and doffed my hat. She looked inside it, unsure.

She buzzed a buzzer on the desk and Lola's unmistakable tones issued from it.

'What?' she snarled in that charming way she has.

'Stan Dawkins to see you, ma'am,' Millie informed her.

'Send him in.'

134

I closed the door of the Mayor's office behind me. 'Twas a first-rate hold and beautifully laid out, like the cabin of a rich buccaneer. Silver was the main colour and all the office equipment, pens and stapler and so forth, were made of it. I wondered if 'twere real. I inspected the underside of a hole-puncher.

'Fingers!' Lola Schwartz said, in her delightful manner.

She was poised behind the desk, like a siren of the ocean ready to lure unwitting sailors on to her rocks. She winked her eye. I winked back. She winked again. I winked back.

'What are you doing?' she asked, sitting a little straighter.

'Responding to your wink,' I said, sliding over and perching myself on the edge of the desk.

'I'm adjusting my contact lens, goofball!'

I smiled and slid into a chair, making a mental note to look up the word goofball.

Lola had called me earlier in the day and being a good and upstanding member of the community, I'd answered her call immediately.

'You're late!' she snapped bewitchingly.

'Trouble with the limo . . .'

'You don't have a limo!'

'Bike, I meant to say. Your hair looks wonderful, if I may say so.'

'No, you may not. Look . . .'

She hurled a wad of papers across the desk at me. I deftly caught them and ran my eye over them. They were minutes from a council meeting.

'Hmmm . . . So Tuppy Jenkins has got his banjo licence back, then. Very interesting.'

Lola sighed and looked up at the ceiling. The ceiling didn't seem to offer any help, so she looked back at me.

'Lower!'

Further down the page something caught my eye, and 'twas something of great importance. I read:

The official opening of the Rockness Monster Rock Festival will take place at 10 p.m. on Friday July 25. Council support will be provided by Police, Ambulance and Sea Scout Brass Band. All council members to attend. Ribbon to be cut by our gracious Mayor, Lola Schwartz.

'So what do you say to that?' she asked, snatching back the papers and slamming them in a drawer.

'I always knew you were gracious!' I said, wiggling my eyebrows irresistibly.

She managed to resist.

'Not that! I meant the date!' She pulled the papers out again and stabbed at them. 'Look July – 25!'

I shrugged. I was never too good on dates.

'That's in two days' time!' she announced.

I nearly fell off the chair. I quickly recovered myself.

'But that's . . . that's . . . two days' time!' I said, playing for time.

Lola came to the front of the desk and leaned against it. I got a whiff of her perfume. 'Twas a heady aroma like the north wind wafting off the palm trees in Jamaica, like the gentle breeze carrying the scent of budding roses across the Moroccan desert, like . . .

'. . . Or you'll never detect in this town again!'

I shook my head, shattering the dream.

'What? Sorry, I drifted off . . .'

Lola craned her neck, bringing her head close to my face.

'Find the Pointy Head Lighthouse by Friday! Understand?'

I nodded. 'Twas a serious matter. I could tell 'twas a serious matter by the serious face Lola was pulling. Her bottom lip was jutting out like a diving board.

I idly toyed with the chair arm.

''Twill be a matter of moments before I have my clammy hands on the lighthouse. My crew and I, as we speak, are hot on the heels of this mysterious mystery . . .'

Lola returned to the other side of the desk. I gulped quietly as she sat in her sumptuous chair and stretched.

'Hot on the heels, huh?'

'Oh, yes.'

'Perhaps you'd care to give me a short run-down on what you've achieved so far.'

I quickly summed up our achievements. Didn't take long.

'So you've got a brick, a door knocker and a ransom note?'

I wasn't going to be defeated so easily. I was about to plunge in and mention the little lighthouse made from the tower of coins, but I bit my lip and took a different tack.

'The ransom note has tooth marks in it, miss!'

I soon found myself on the steps of the town hall. Lola was right behind me as she marched me through the doors and on to the steps. She gave me a hearty push, brushed her hands, yelled 'Friday!' and then slammed the door in my face.

I played with the ransom note as it lay on the wonky coffee table and thought about the brick and the door knocker. The case was proving itself a wily and weird one. The clues were scant and the end of this particular voyage was still far over the horizon. Spot sat on my shoulder and we both sighed together.

Suddenly and without warning Spot fell backwards and landed with a plop on the settee. I turned to my little feathery friend.

'Spot, Spot, squawk to me!'

Spot jumped up and squawked.

I was confuddled by his behaviour.

'Pull yourself together, Spot!' I ordered. 'This is a time to think. Think!'

Spot squawked again and once more threw himself into a faint. Whatever was the mad bird a-doing?

'Has Ho been putting grog in your water?'

At that Spot shook his little head, picked up a sunflower seed in his beak and spat it at me. I grabbed him by his little neck and pointed my threatening finger at him.

'If you don't behave – you'll be back in the sock drawer!'

Then a thought occurred. 'Twas but a small thought at first, but it soon grew into a fully formed thought and arrived with a fanfare in my head.

'You're being Long John Saliva!'

Spot sighed. The message had got across. He

nodded eagerly as further thoughts were coaxed from my addled brain.

'You're being Long John Saliva fainting . . .'

Spot clapped his wings and hopped excitedly.

'And Long John fainted when I was talking to Ho . . .'

Spot was skipping around in a circle, nodding his head madly.

'Long John Saliva fainted when he heard the little lighthouse was worth £1,750,000!'

'Cock-a-doodle-doo!!'

Spot squawked and fell on his back, breathless.

I gazed down at him.

'You don't have to do it again. I get the point!' I stroked my grizzled chin. 'Twas time for decisive action. I decisively reached for the remote control.

The television picture shimmered into view. 'Twas my favourite show, *Police Watch*. Maybe I could glean some tricks from it. As I stared at the screen, I slowly realized I was about to glean a lot.

In the picture was Joe 'Greasy' Spoon, the very solicitor who had taken on the case of Moll. He was sat on a sofa and by his side was Bootleg Bess. Whatever was a-happening?

A tanned interviewer was poking one of those micronophones towards Bess.

'So tell us your tale, Bess.'

Bootleg was clutching a hankie and dabbing her eyes occasionally. This is what she said.

'It was a horrible moment. I was walking home from my evening doing charity work . . . I help out at Dunpaddling, the old sailors' home . . . when, from the darkness, a stranger swooped on me, pushed me to the ground and . . . and . . .'

She dabbed some more.

'Go on!' said the interviewer.

'And nibbled my ear!' She blew her nose loudly.

'Maybe I should take over,' interrupted 'Greasy', pointing at Bess's leather ear.

'And here are the nibble marks, still left in my poor client's ear.'

The camera zoomed in like an eagle on its prey.

'These are the tell-tale tooth marks . . .'

'And there's something very special about these tooth marks, isn't there, Joe? Perhaps you could tell us in your own words.'

'Greasy' pointed an accusing finger at the leather ear.

'Yes, these tooth marks are precisely the same tooth marks as those found all over town the other night.'

The interviewer gasped and looked into the camera.

'So you mean to say—'

141

'My client, Bootleg Bess, had her ear nibbled by none other than the dastardly criminal Molly Meakins!'

The interviewer smiled at the camera.

'Though she's locked up, is Molly Meakins the naughty nibbler of this ear? In part two – the tooth, the whole tooth and nothing but the tooth!'

The theme music wobbled into my ears as I flicked off the TV.

Molly? Dastardly? Nibbling Bess's ear? What fish swill is this? And when did Bess become a client of 'Greasy'? I thought he was working on behalf of Moll?

This was proving a tempestuous voyage. I scribbled some notes:

> Moll in jail for putting tooth marks all about town. And now accused of nibbling Bootleg Bess's ear.
> Long John Saliva behaving suspiciously.
> A lost lighthouse and a keeper who keeps arguing with himself.
> Roman coins worth £1,750,000.
> A door knocker from the lighthouse.
> And a ransom note with Moll's tooth marks in it . . .
> Wherever will it all end?

Chapter Twelve

Time was nipping at my flippers. Two days was all we had left to solve this case, but old Sam Hawkins refused to be scuppered. Sam Hawkins, who once swam two leagues with a mouth full of maggots. The Pointy Head Lighthouse was to be unveiled this very Friday, as the centrepiece of the new festival stadium, but unfortunately 'twas nowhere to be seen. I gazed out of the window of the Naughty Lass. Far in the distance I could just see bobbling boats in the Washed-up Harbour, their masts a-waving like the hands of a classroom of children who all know the answer.

A knock came to my bedroom door, dredging my thoughts from the depths of concentration. Little Ho's face peeked around the corner.

'What is the meaning of this interruption? I was mid-think, Ho!'

But Ho did not respond with his usual jaunty wit. Oh, no, he merely beckoned me with a finger, while another was pressed to his lips. Something was amiss and I silently crept behind him as he led me from my hold.

Bleep-bleeping noises were emerging from the cellar. Bleep-bleeping interrupted by gurgles of giggles and the occasional slurp. 'Twas Long John Saliva. What was the old sea dog a-doing now? We crept towards the door and placed our shell-likes to the key-hole.

I whispered to Ho, 'What's he up to?'

Ho shrugged.

'He sounds like he's playing with our computer. I recognize the bleeping.'

And that's where we keep all our secret detecting files, I thought. Right!

I decided to challenge our guest. He'd been shifty and strange of late and 'twas time to put my suspicions to the test. I would confront him, challenge him and, if necessary, fight a duel. I'd not duelled for a long time, but I hadn't lost my touch. 'Twas merely a matter of making sure the other duellist had the shorter sword. I would smash open the door, charge in and have it out with him. I let Spot go first, then followed him in with a hearty, 'Aha!'

'Twas then I tripped on the top step, tumbled down

the entire flight of stairs and landed with my arms in two large vases at the bottom. I stood up and found a biscuit tin wedged on my head. I tried to recover the situation by nodding the wretched tin off my head. It wouldn't shift. Ho saw my dilemma, seized the barrel and prised it from my head with an almost audible pop.

Long John swivelled his head as I made my entrance and looked me up and down as I tried to brush down my jacket. I couldn't, of course, because each of my arms was in a vase.

I pointed one at him accusingly.

'Aha!' I said, unsure what else to add.

'Yes, you said that,' replied Long John, turning his lanky body to face me, masking the computer screen. 'What do you want?'

I nodded towards the computer.

'That!' I said at last. 'What are you doing with that?'

Long John followed my gaze and it landed on the computer behind him. He smiled.

'Oh, that. I was just emailing an old friend of mine in the Med. You remember Capsize Kate?'

'Yes!' I said, clutching at straws. 'Didn't she used to make the finest ship's biscuits on the south coast?'

'No, she didn't – she used to make hats. That's why we called her *Cap*size Kate. Finest hat maker in Portsmouth, old Kate.'

I tried to be as casual as possible, but I had to see the computer screen.

'Capsize Kate, of course, I must have been a-thinking of another Kate . . .'

I moved towards the computer and, just as I was about to see what was on the screen, Long John spat a cherry stone at the power button and switched it off.

'That's it!' I suddenly shouted, 'I've had it up to here!' I gestured to my neck – difficult to do when your hand is in a vase. 'You turn up on our doorstep, unannounced, you ask me for money, you eat up all our vittles without offering to pay, and now I find you snooping through our computer files. Well, Long John Saliva, 'tis time to weigh your anchor and leave!'

I stood and pointed to the stairs – difficult to do when your hand is still in a vase.

Long John snarled and a little angry spittle dribbled down his chin. Ho had crept back up the stairs and was quaking at the top, but as I glanced at him he gave me a thumbs-up sign.

Within minutes Long John was on the doorstep of the Naughty Lass, his bag in his hand and a huffing look on his face.

'But we're old bilge-room buddies, you and I!' he pleaded.

''Tis too late, Long John. You've battered your cod, now you must eat it!' I pointed towards the outside

world – difficult to do when your hand is still in a vase.
'Sling your anchor!'

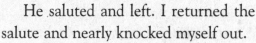

'Very well!' he snarled once more.
'But I'll never forget this, Hawkins! If
ever you run aground, if ever you're
stranded, if ever you're cast adrift,
don't come paddling to me!'

He saluted and left. I returned the
salute and nearly knocked myself out.

Long John Saliva stomped down the driveway, his
bag slung over his shoulder, huffing and puffing like a
steam boat.

Suddenly, from out of nowhere, Spot the Parrot
launched himself down the drive at a rare rate of
knots. He swooped down on Long John, poked his little head into the pirate's coat pocket and retrieved
something. Spot was a highly experienced pickpocket
and Long John didn't notice a thing. He fluttered back
to me, tried to drop his catch in my hand, but finding
my hand otherwise engaged, gave it to Ho.

'Our house keys!' announced Ho, brightly waving
the jellyfish keyring I'd bought him for his birthday.
'One from the front door and one from the safe. He
was trying to steal them!'

'Well done, Spot!' I cried with delight. I would
have clapped too, but, well, you understand.

I turned and re-entered the Naughty Lass.

'Ho,' I said, 'fetch a hammer!'

Ho was tipping the remains of the broken vases into the dustbin when he let out a merry whoop and came running into the lounge.

'Do you want to see what I've just done by the litter bin?'

'Not really,' I said, inspecting the door knocker through a magnifying glass.

'Well, I'll show it to you here, then!'

Ho flicked on a nearby lamp, pointed it at the wall and started fiddling his fingers in the beam.

'Can you see what it is?' he asked eagerly.

'It's a donkey . . . a cat . . . a small vole . . . No, it's a jar of chutney!'

'No!' he yelled indignantly.

'The Great Wall of China?' I suggested with a shrug.

'It's a soaring eagle, dumbo!'

'Probably best to stick to doing the bunny. You did a very good bunny, Ho!'

The phone tinkled into life as Ho made a rude silhouette gesture and left the room.

'Sam Hawkins, award-winning Pirate Detective!'

'I have a pebble in my ear!'

'Twas Billy Buddy. I lowered my nautical rump on the settee and sighed.

'You've got a what?' I said quietly.

'Pardon?' came the reply.

'You've . . . got . . . a . . . what?' I shouted at the phone.

'I can't hear you – I've got a pebble in my ear. Wait, I'll hand you over.'

Billy's second voice spoke next. *'I've got a pebble in my ear!'*

'How did that happen?'

'Pardon?'

'Oh, never mind. I'd better come over.'

'Pardon?'

'What did he say?' said the first voice.

'I don't know,' said the second, *'I've got a pebble in my ear.'*

I gently replaced the receiver and shrugged.

'Ho!' I bellowed. 'Fetch some soap and a cotton-bud. We've got a job to do!'

Within minutes Ho and I had moored the Nippy Clipper outside the Red Sea Lion Tavern and found ourselves inside room 6.

Billy Buddy was a-sitting on his little bed, frantically pointing at his ear. I calmed him down and Ho and I took a cotton-bud and prised the pebble from his shell-like.

Pop!

'Thank you!' said Billy.

'*Thank you!*' said Billy.

I sat on the bed next to him and placed a comforting arm about his shoulders.

'Now, tell me how this happened.'

'I was walking along the promenade this morning to find some breakfast. And I thought I might take a photo of myself with my new gadget.'

From inside his dungarees he pulled a slim mobile phone. Now, I know you can't take photos with a phone, but Billy was a little dotty.

'Wow!' said Ho. 'It's one of those new video phones. You can take photos with these. Can I have one, Sam? Can I, can I?'

I took the video phone and inspected it.

'Ah . . .' I said, 'a video phone, that is. Where do you put the tapes in?'

'No, it's like a camera. Click-clicks!'

'So there I was, posing by the pier, my mobile in my hand, and just as I took the picture a pebble hit me in the ear!'

Strange, I thought, but then another thought dropped anchor in my mental harbour.

'Maybe there's a clue in the photograph. Come, crew, we must go to the chemist's and get this phone developed!'

Ho tugged at my sleeve as I leapt to my feet.

'It's digital!'

'It's digital!' I announced, and sat down again.

Billy Buddy opened the phone and we all gazed at the little screen. Nothing was what we saw. He stabbed at a couple of buttons and nothing was what we saw again.

'Oh, give it to me!' he said, and changed hands.

A picture faded into being. 'Twas old Billy Buddy himself, standing, as he said, before the Grand Washed-up Pier. But nothing else. No clue, no tell-tale clue. Blowholes!

'Wait!' shrieked Ho. 'Look!' And he pointed towards a small speck on the picture. 'It's a pebble!'

And my little Oriental pal was right. 'Twas the pebble we'd just squeezed from Billy's ear, caught by the camera in mid-flight. 'Twas a clue, a tell-tale clue!

'And if you look really carefully, what can you see?'

I looked really carefully.

'Hmmm . . .' I concluded.

'There's a trail of spit coming off the back of it!'

He was right once again. What a clever cabin boy, very well trained. I studied the photo once more. There seemed to be a tiny comet heading towards Billy's head.

'And there's only one person who could spit a pebble with such deadly accuracy! Long John Saliva!'

I was still a little confuddled.

151

'But why would Long John attack him?' I said, pointing at Billy.

'*Or me?*' said Billy, pointing at himself.

Ho's face lit up.

'Because Long John knows the little lighthouse is worth £1,750,000!'

'But the little lighthouse is in the Naughty Lass's safe!' I replied, nibbling a knuckle as I thought.

'But Long John doesn't know that. He must have thought Billy still had it! That's why he attacked him.' Then Ho placed a hand on both our shoulders and a dark expression seized his face. 'But he'll soon work out where it is, and when he does – he'll be back!'

All four of us gulped.

Later that day in the Naughty Lass, myself, Ho and Spot were celebrating our success when a ping came to the ship's bell. And when the ship's bell pings like that, it can only mean one thing.

'Long John Saliva!' we chorused, and scuttled down the corridor to the front door.

I threw it open to find a sad and lonely face.

'Please take me back,' pleaded Long John. 'No one else will have me. I've been to Dunpaddling, but they only take party bookings these days. I've tried to get a room at the Red Sea Lion, the Benbow, the Black Spot and the Jolly Otter, but they're all full because of the Rockness Monster Rock Festival . . .'

As he was saying this, he slowly started to slide himself through the door. I held up a hand to stop him.

'Heave-ho a mo, Long John. Do you recognize this?'

And with that I held up the pebble we'd prised from Billy Buddy's ear not one hour before.

The sad face of Long John Saliva, the penniless musician, suddenly became the furious face of Long John Saliva, the captured barracuda.

'Pah! So, Sam Hawkins, you think you've caught me, do you?'

'More or less!'

'I shall have the little lighthouse and all it's worth – when I find it!'

I held up the keyring and jangled it before his startled face.

'Ha! You should have looked in the safe while you had the chance!'

Long John swiped at the keys, but I whipped them away before he could grab them. I slammed the door shut. Ho, Spot and I peered through the letter box as he leapt over the fence and ran off down Puddle Lane.

'Do you think we should have grabbed him?' asked Ho.

'Ah . . . . . .' I replied.

Chapter Thirteen

Clump Tower was a thunderingly tall building and 'twas golden as well. Twinkling sunlight glinted off the windows and winked at passers-by. But 'twas not the merry place it seemed from the outside. Within was a hissing nest of money makers, company owners and corporate thugs, all led by the enterprising entrepreneur and quadrillionaire Harvey Clump. 'Twas he who owned and controlled every important business in Washed-upon-the-Beach, from the Lobster King chain of fast-food outlets to Larry Limpet's shoe-shine stall, from Leisure Island, the giant theme park, to Mr Whimpley's Tip of the Ice-cream Van. He even owned the *Daily Splash* and the local TV and radio station. And 'twas he who was mounting the Rockness Monster Rock Festival, with the Pointy Head Lighthouse as its central attraction. Now Harvey Clump had claimed that he didn't steal

the lighthouse, but there was only one way to find out the truth. To enter Clump Tower.

Ho, Spot and I stood on the pavement outside the huge building like three new boys meeting the school bully for the first time. We looked up at the building and gulped. 'Twas at least thirty storeys high.

I took a deep breath and control of my crew.

'Now, then, maties, herein lies our destiny, our future and the end of our case. The answers to our mystery are inside that building. Climb aboard, crew! It could be a choppy voyage!'

We braced ourselves, shook hands and walked towards the rotating door. Within seconds we were rotated out again by a large, tall thug with sunglasses and a surprisingly wide head.

'Get out! No one sees Mr Clump without an appointment!'

I quickly gathered my nautical wits.

'I'd like an appointment, please!' I said.

'No one gets an appointment without an appointment!'

He dusted off his black jacket and rotated back into the building.

Ho helped me to my feet.

'So how are we going to get in, smartie pants?'

I was pleased Ho liked my new trousers, but he really must concentrate on the case.

'Twas at this point my seagull eye spotted our saviour. There, moored on the other side of the street, was a small white van. Lettering on its side read 'Weed All About It'. The back door seemed to be open and out poked gloves, masks, spray cans and a hose.

I quickly looked from side to side, then beckoned my crew.

'Old Sam has a plan. Follow me, boys.'

Three masked figures lurched through the rotating doors of Clump Tower, all brandishing spray cans and one twirling a hose. And how do I know this? Because it was us! What a cunning plot I was a-hatching.

I pounded over to the receptionist, quickly flashed my library card and then snatched it away before she could read it.

'I am Angus Fungus from Weed All About It. We have just received a terrifying report from our coastal lookout that a swarm of the deadly Bladderwrack Bug has headed inland. And its first port of call is to be Clump Tower. Somewhere in this building there is a Bladderwrack Bug.'

The lady gazed over her glasses like a goldfish straining to look out of the bowl.

'Sign in, please.'

'No time!' shrieked Ho. 'This is a serious business.

If you get bitten by a Bladderwrack Bug, your ears turn green and your nose falls off. Everyone knows that!'

Spot wiggled his hose in the background to support Ho's claim.

The receptionist took the bait. Ha!

'What should I do?' she asked, starting to sound nervous.

Ha! Once more my sweaty palm was on the tiller of this mystery. I leaned across the counter and spoke slowly.

'Evacute the building!'

She looked around and swiftly spotted a red knob by the desk. She swatted it like a fly.

The shrill alarm cut through the building like a rudder through water. Within seconds people were pouring from every emergency exit like maggots from a bucket.

I adjusted my mask, held my spray can aloft and announced, 'Now to find the bug!'

We entered the lift.

'Where would we like to go today?'

I looked about, but saw only Ho and Spot.

'No time for pranks, Ho, press the button for Harvey Clump's office!'

Ho and Spot stared at each other. Neither had spoken.

We all looked about, a little unsure. The voice returned.

'Where would we like to go today?'

'Twas a strange mechanical voice.

'Who said that?' I asked, looking about the lift. It didn't take long.

'I'm sorry, I didn't comprehend your answer. Where would we like to go today?'

'Twas the lift itself talking. A strange world we live in.

'Harvey Clump's office,' I said slowly.

'Very well. Harvey Clump's office. Going up!' And then it started to coun: '1 . . . 2 . . . 3 . . . 4 . . .'

I clutched my spray can closer to my chest and looked down at my hearty crew. If only Moll were here to complete the complement. 'Twas an odd voyage with a missing crewman.

'10 . . . 11 . . . 12 . . . 13 . . . 14 . . .'

We stood silently as the elevator ascended this mighty building.

'. . . 22 . . . 23 . . . 24 . . . 25 . . .'

Somewhere in this building was the information that would solve our meddlesome mystery and restore my reputation as the finest pirate detective ever to tramp the streets of Washed-upon-the-Beach.

'Ping! Floor 30,' said the lift.

'Thank you!' I replied, then realized I was addressing a machine.

'Don't mention it,' answered the lift, as the doors

slid softly shut.

We turned to investigate our surroundings.

We pitter-pattered along the carpeted corridor – all was silent as the deep. Not a sole to be seen. People had left their work hastily. Computers bleeped, papers were spread about, staplers sat unused and hole-punchers did not punch. We snooped back and forth. But which was Harvey Clump's office?

Suddenly, Ho hissed.

'Boss!' He excitedly beckoned Spot and me over. 'This is Harvey Clump's office, Sam!'

'Brilliant, Ho. How did you know?'

He pointed to the big red sign on the door:

HARVEY CLUMP'S OFFICE
NEVER KNOCK!

I pressed my shell-like to the door and I heard giggling. Giggling and the clink of glasses. A male voice and a female voice.

At that point Spot dropped his hose. It slapped loudly on Ho's foot. I tore my head from the door and hissed.

'Quiet, we're on to something!'

I returned my ear to the door. Well, I thought I was returning my ear to the door. But now the door seemed a little softer – silky soft in fact – with a button in the

159

middle, and it was breathing in and out. I gulped and stood up.

Before me was Harvey Clump, the richest, most powerful man in Washed-upon-the-Beach.

'Angus Fungus!' I gibbered. 'Ermmm . . . Bladderwrack Bug . . . erm . . . all over the place . . . best evacuate!'

'This office is uniquely equipped with the finest fire-proof, bug-repellent, anti-burglar devices currently on the market!' said Harvey, gesturing all over his office. 'I need to protect my precious guests!'

Then came a voice I recognized.

'Sam Hawkins? Is that you!'

The beauteous face of Lola Schwartz hove into view from behind Clump. So she was Clump's precious guest, but what was she doing here?

She answered my quizzical look.

'Harvey was just showing me the model of the new stadium. It's great.'

She suddenly grabbed me by the hand and pulled me into the office. I glided past a silent but deadly Clump. Ho and Spot followed behind, doffing their masks.

Clump slammed the door.

'Do you know these jerks?'

Jerk? Jerk? Didn't he know who I was?

'Sir, I am not a jerk. I am Sam Hawkins, Pirate

Detective. I have sailed the seven seas . . .'

Clump strode over to me, leaned to one side and turned his head upside down.

'Don't I know you from somewhere?'

Ho leapt betwixt me and the businessman.

'Probably seen his face in the paper.'

Clump pushed Ho out of the way and he nearly squashed Spot.

'You're the one who tried to climb into my limo the other day.'

I clawed my brain to find a clever bluff. I found one.

'No, you must be thinking of my brother . . . Pam!'

Ho realized the situation could only get worse so suddenly he yelled, 'What a lovely model!'

In the confusion I had failed to notice a large model in the centre of Clump's desk.

'Isn't it cute?' agreed Lola.

We gathered round it like tadpole catchers round a pond.

I noticed Clump slip his arm around Lola slightly.

'Yes, indeedy. This is gonna be *the* greatest rock festival in the history of Washed-upon-the-Beach!'

He gave us a swift guided tour, pointing out the potential income it would generate for him. Then he pointed to the Pointy

Head Lighthouse.

'And dominating the whole scene will be this wonderful old artefact, restored to its former splendour by the finest craftsman in town.'

Lola dropped a beady eye on me.

'Once we get it back.'

I fingered my neckerchief.

''Tis only a matter of time, before—'

My speech was interrupted by a tapping on the window. Spot, for reasons best known to himself, was banging his hose against it.

'Not now, Spot. The Pointy Head Lighthouse will soon be—'

Tap-tap-tap . . .

Ho ran over to see what Spot was tapping about.

'Boss!' he cried.

'Not now, Ho. The Pointy Head Lighthouse will soon be . . .'

Lola and Harvey joined Ho and Spot at the window. Lola was pointing and giggling gleefully.

'Look, it's a little brass band!'

She slid open the glass panel.

I heard the trumpeting and banging as the band drew closer, but I tried to continue with my tale.

'. . . will soon be in our grasp . . .'

'Look at their cute little uniforms!'

'Sea Scouts!' said Ho, smiling up at Lola.

'They're so cute!'

The band was getting even louder now. Louder and closer.

Harvey placed his hand on Lola's shoulder.

'Do you like them, honey? Would you like me to buy them for you? Would you?'

Honey?

Lola placed her hand on Clump's hand.

'You are so sweet!'

I started to stomp towards Lola and Clump. This was no time for romantic whittering – I had a case to solve. But Spot's hose was curled on the floor. It snaked around my ankle and snagged my leg in mid-stride. I tripped and fell face first on to the model.

CRUNCH!

'Twas indeed a crunch. A crunch of my head on the little model. But 'twas also a crunch followed by a crash. And the crash was followed by a tinkle-tinkle. I looked up, brushing model AstroTurf from my fore-head, to see four startled faces staring through a shattered office window.

'What the—' said Clump.

I ran to the window. Seems upon slapping my nautical forehead on the model I had inadvertently launched the little model lighthouse into the air and

163

sent it careering out of the window. I hope it landed on something soft.

I peeked out. Thirty floors below, Able Seaman Christopher Wave lay flat out on the tarmac with a model lighthouse in his stomach. He was surrounded by a gaggle of Sea Scouts clutching their brass instruments. They looked down at their leader, then they all slowly turned and looked up at me. I waved a nervous wave at Wave and withdrew as they started shaking their instruments threateningly.

'Twas a nice summer's day as four heavy thugs bundled us from Clump Tower. We landed with a thump on the pavement. I stood up, reshaped my hat and addressed the crew.

'Gentlemen, I think we should return to the Naughty Lass.'

'But, boss, what about the case?' asked Ho.

'But, Ho,' I replied, 'what about the Sea Scouts?' I pointed towards the gaggle of angry faces that were slowly approaching.

'Run!'

And we launched ourselves into a mad dash for home.

We eeled and snaked our way through the back streets of Washed-upon-the-Beach and before long had managed to shake off the Sea Scouts. With relief we drew into the welcoming harbour of the Naughty Lass.

Chapter Fourteen

The waiting room to Joe 'Greasy' Spoon's office was like a dry dock festooned with snappy shots of past successes. Photographs covered the walls and from out of each one sneered the untrustworthy face of Spoon. Three tatty chairs nestled around a small wooden table covered with dusty magazines. We had been summoned by the slimy solicitor and sat twiddling our thumbs. We wondered what the turncoat had in store for us.

Ho was biding his time, looking through the cuttings and photos on the wall.

'"Local Lawyer Saves Duck from the Dock!"' he quoted, then, '"Radish Thief Proved Not Guilty by Spoon! Spoon Butters the Jury!" Wow, this guy is really good!'

'Shouldn't that last one read "Spoon *Batters* the Jury"?'

'No, it was butters!' said a voice that wasn't Ho's. 'Dreadful case about industrial espionage in a margarine factory. I had to butter up the jury to prove a point!' Spoon had slunk in the waiting room and answered my question.

'And did you get a unanimous verdict?' I asked.

'Well, it was a fair spread.'

He stepped up to me and shook my hand. 'Twas like holding a bunch of frozen fish fingers.

I decided 'twas best to get down to business immediately. I adjusted Spot on my shoulder and spoke.

'Why have you called us here, Spoon?'

Spoon sat opposite me and I watched his rodent-like features as they scuttled about his face and finally composed themselves.

'Mr Hawkins . . .' he began.

'Call me Sam. We've ploughed many a tempest together, you and I. Old seagoing pals always use first names, matey. It proves their lifelong bond of honour!'

'Mr Hawkins,' he continued, 'as you know, my client, Molly Meakins, has been charged with breaking and entering properties throughout Washed-upon-the-Beach and leaving tooth marks in various objects.'

I crossed my arms and huffed. Spot crossed his wings and huffed too. Ho looked on, eager to hear more.

'Piffle and tush!' I said. 'Moll is no criminal. She is

as honest as young Ho here!' I gestured at Ho, who was quietly sneaking a stapler into his pocket.

Spoon coughed. 'Mr Hawkins, the evidence is incontrovertible . . .'

'Well, that's all right, then,' I said, and got up.

Spoon coughed again. 'Incontrovertible means it cannot be disproved!'

I sat down again as Spoon continued. 'Look . . .'

He produced three large plastic sacks, each of which contained a sample.

'Mrs Clack's Lemon Pie – tooth marks. Mr Plimple's new-laid lawn – tooth marks. The exhaust pipe of Bishop Whippy's new car – tooth marks!' He wiggled each object under my nose as he spoke.

I brushed them aside.

'Pah and tush, I say, matey!'

Spoon coughed again. 'Molly Meakins is undoubtedly guilty, Mr Hawkins. I am going to lose the case. If I lose the case, I lose money. And I do not like to lose money. So I have covered myself. I am also representing one Bootleg Bess, who has accused Ms Meakins of nibbling her ear.'

'Is that legal?' interrupted Ho. 'I mean, representing two different sides in the same case?'

Spoon patted him on his head. He winced.

'Legal? Of course it's legal. Sweet child!'

Ho moved out of arm's reach and sat by the door.

'Two clients in one case? Trying to catch two pilchards with one net, eh? I think you've nibbled off more than you can munch, Greasy!' I shouted. 'What kind of country are we living in where someone can't have a little nibble now and then without breaking the law?'

Spoon coughed, once more.'It's not the nibbling, Mr Hawkins – it's the breaking and entering, and, in the case of Bootleg Bess, it's a matter of common assault. However, there is one hope. A chink of sunlight in this sad case.'

'And what is that, matey?' I asked, inching myself forward on the chair.

'Tomorrow I intend to hold an identity parade. If Bootleg Bess fails to recognize the teeth that nibbled her ear, then there may be hope. However, if she *does* recognize the teeth, then Molly Meakins could be looking at a prison sentence of six years.'

Six years! But that's madness. Old Moll banged up during the best years of her life. Something was wrong, very wrong. I had to prove Moll innocent and save my little pal from a fate worse than Ho's cooking.

The game was afin!

Back at the Naughty Lass the phone tinkled into life and I snatched it from its jingling cradle.

'Sam Hawkins, award-winning Pirate Detective!' I announced brightly.

'Where's the lighthouse?' asked a familiar voice.

'Lola!' I said, my own voice trembling slightly. 'I was just cleaning the parrot cage and thinking of you.'

'How sweet. Where's the lighthouse?'

'Ah, you impetuous maid. 'Tis but a matter of time before I haul our prize into harbour, safe and sound.'

'You've no idea, have you?'

'Well, it wouldn't be fair to say I have no—'

'Where's the lighthouse?'

'I've no idea.'

Curses and cuttlefish! I'd crumbled under her clever questioning. The cold fact was laid out on the slab like a well-filleted halibut. I had no idea where the lighthouse was.

'Friday – Grand Opening of the Rockness Monster Rock Festival!' said Lola flatly, and hung up.

Then there was a tapping at the front door. I replaced the phone and padded down the corridor. As I threw open the door I saw a familiar face.

'Hawkins, me old shipmate, me old corking pal, me old—'

'Long John, what do you want back here?'

He had a jaunty grin across his grizzled face and for one fleeting moment I lowered my guard. I stood back to let him through and 'twas like opening the floodgates. Long John smashed the door against the wall and stomped in.

I was about to make a witty remark when he grabbed me by the neckerchief and pushed me towards the wall. A little brass anchor fell off its hook and clattered on to the deck.

'I'll tell you what I want!'

Spot fluttered into the room and landed on Long John's shoulder. He was about to peck at the pirate's ear when Long John grabbed him with his other hand and pushed him against the wall next to me.

'I want to know how you are going to prove I attacked Billy Buddy.'

I gurgled an answer, but Long John's grip was too tight around my throat.

'You may have a picture of a pebble in the air,' he snarled, 'you may a picture of some spittle, but you don't have a picture of me in the photograph. Do you? Evidence! Proof! You have nothing!'

At which point Ho entered with a magnifying glass to his eye and the photograph in his hand. So engaged was he with the picture he'd failed to notice the scene before him.

'Look, boss, if you hold this magnifying glass really close you can see Long John's face just in the corner . . .'

He looked up, smiled, gulped, squealed and tried to run off. Long John dropped Spot and grabbed Ho by the tail of his tunic. He drew the boy towards him. There was nothing I could do to help. Long John leaned across, snatched the photo from Ho's hand and released us both.

He steamed towards the door, but paused on the threshold.

'Thank you, gentlemen – you've made my job very easy!'

He slammed the door and was gone.

Oh, molluscs! I thought, as I sat quaffing a frothy grog later that day. Oh, barnacles! I was making a squid's dinner of this case, once again. I'd lost the finest piece of evidence we had for convicting Long John Saliva. Molly was still in jail. I had no idea who the Scarlet Winkle was. The Pointy Head Lighthouse was still missing.

What was an old salt to do? In all my maritime years I'd never been so flummoxed and confuddled by a mystery. And with the Rockness Monster Rock Festival only a day away I was up the rigging with a paddle.

I licked a little froth from my thumb and pondered.

Who was the Scarlet Winkle? Why would he steal a lighthouse? Where would he put it? Questions swirled through my brain but the answers went down the plughole.

And tomorrow old Moll would be found guilty of a crime I knew she didn't commit. Tomorrow she would be put away for six years.

I stood up and called my crew together.

''Tis a sad time in our voyage, but we must muster our courage and visit our sister sailor for one final farewell!'

Ho and Spot saluted and we headed for the door.

'Twas a sad and depressing walk along the prom that afternoon. Dark clouds were gathering overhead and the seagulls seemed to be squawking a warning of an impending storm.

Ho, Spot and I traipsed towards the Washed-upon-the-Beach prison, knowing our old shipmate might be slammed in the clinker for a very long time. Whatever could we say to her? What words of solace and hope could we offer? I glanced at Ho. A tear glistened on his cheek and Spot had dipped his beak in respect.

We made ourselves known to the officer in charge and went inside.

173

The door to Moll's cell slid open and sadly we crept in.

'Whoopppppeeeee!'

There was a yell of delight and a cracker exploded. The cell was festooned with festive decorations. What nonsense was this?

Moll was dancing in the centre of the room with an Old Spice Girl on either side.

'It's our berthday!' they chorused as we entered. 'Did you bring a bottle?'

We gazed about, unable to take it all in.

I pointed at the Old Spice Girls.

'But I thought you'd escaped!' I said, over the music.

'We got caught again! It happens most weeks.' They giggled and danced away.

Moll was holding a plate under my nose.

'Would you like a chocolate hob-nob? Or would you like to join me in a bop?'

I couldn't believe my eyes. The day before she was due to be sentenced and Moll was boogieing away to pop music.

'Have some jelly instead!'

I clicked off the seedy CD and addressed the party: 'Moll, you are in court tomorrow. The evidence against you is uncomfort . . . inedible . . .'

'Incontrovertible!' helped Ho.

'Incontrovertible – you are looking at a sentence of six years!'

Molly continued dancing, despite my words and lack of music.

'Molly!'

She wobbled to a halt.

'No, I'm not,' she announced, slurping on a lemonade.

We were confused. Spot shrugged and shook his little head.

'Not what?' I asked slowly.

'I'm not going away for six years. In fact, after tomorrow I don't think I'll be going anywhere except home!'

She started to dance again, but stopped when she saw my confused expression.

'But you have left tooth marks all over town.'

'No, I haven't!'

'There's piles of evidence. Your teeth are guilty teeth!'

'My teeth might be guilty, but I'm not!'

And with that she poked her fingers into her grotty gob, slipped her gnashers from her mouth and snapped them a couple of times before my bewildered face.

Moll had false teeth!

'Anyone could have thtolen them, Tham!' She slipped the teeth back in and translated: 'Anyone

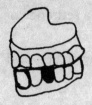
could have stolen them, Sam.'

Of course! Why hadn't I thought of that before? Moll *was* innocent! Her teeth were merely accomplices. Ha! And double ha!

I switched the music back on and the boogieing recommenced. I watched as my merry crew gyrated to the beat, but one thought was nagging at the depths of my mind like a cheeky tuna nipping a whale's tail.

Who had stolen Molly's false teeth?

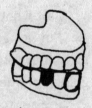

Chapter Fifteen

O n the wall in the police station a solemn clock looked down on me, Ho, Spot and 'Greasy' Spoon and tick-tocked away. In the stark room were four stools in a row and on each one, except the last, sat a lonely pair of false teeth. 'Twas the identity parade and Molly's false gnashers were the prime suspects.

Spoon was flicking through his papers with an oily smile on his face. No matter what the outcome of this case, he was a winner. Ho sighed and stared at the ceiling, and Spot tapped his little claw in time to the tick-tocking of the clock.

Eventually, a key turned in the door, bolts slid back and Molly entered the room. Her hands were cuffed to an officer, but she was not downhearted. She giggled and gave us a little wave that almost snatched the officer from his feet.

Spoon stepped forward and addressed her. 'Molly Meakin, please remove your teeth.'

Molly slipped her dirty fingers into her cavernous mouth and, with a sloppy slurp, withdrew her false teeth. She smiled with a mouth like a squid's bottom. Spoon gingerly took the teeth and placed them on the fourth stool.

The clock continued its tick-tock as we waited once more in silence.

At the far end of the room another door creaked open and we all turned towards it. Framed in the doorway was a figure whose face was draped in a black veil. 'Twas Bootleg Bess, the victim of the crime Molly never committed. She entered slowly and cautiously. In fact, she entered a little *too* slowly and cautiously. She looked like she was paddling barefoot in a pool of angry crabs.

As she arrived at the stools Spoon patted her on the shoulder and lifted her veil. She let out a wail of anguish and fluttered a handkerchief across her forehead. This was the performance of an artist used to melting the hardiest of hearts for her own devious ends. Spoon spoke gently to her.

'Now, Miss Leg, I'm sure you know why you are here.'

Bootleg nodded, sniffed and did her finest upset expression.

'I am going to take each set of false teeth and nibble your ear!'

Another wail erupted from the black-hearted spinster. 'Twas clear to any old sole this was a put-on by a experienced show-off.

'Brace yourself, Miss Leg. You must be brave. Once you recognize the teeth that nibbled you, I want you to hold up your hand. Do you understand?'

Bootleg nodded and Spoon escorted her to the first pair of teeth. She pushed her hair behind her ear as he picked them up. Very carefully, he applied the teeth to her ear and gave it the tiniest of nibbles. Bess suddenly tittered like a naughty schoolgirl. The teeth were removed and her titter evaporated. She shook her head solemnly and they moved to the next pair. Once again the teeth were applied to her ear, once again she tittered and once again she shook her head. When the third pair was tried, she shook her head. And then they approached Molly's teeth.

Spot flew to my shoulder and hugged my ear. Ho held my arm. We watched anxiously. Molly's smile seemed to have disappeared too.

Spoon carefully took the pair from the stool, held them between his fingers and applied them to Bootleg's ear. She tittered madly, her body quivered like a sneezing jellyfish, Spoon removed the teeth and the quivering stopped. We waited with baited breath.

Ho clenched my arm and I felt Spot trembling on my shoulder. Bess slowly looked up at us and then at Molly. She lifted her hand in the air.

'These are the teeth that nibbled me!' she blared, then wailed like the winner of a siren-blowing competition and fled from the room.

Spoon replaced the teeth on the stool and spoke.

'Molly Meakin, this is incontrovertible evidence that you nibbled Bootleg Bess's ear. You will now go for sentencing and will be put away for a very long time!' He could hardly contain his glee.

Molly was having none of this. She stomped over to the solicitor, dragging the police officer behind her. We all leapt aboard her and tried to restrain her from grabbing him by the neck.

'Thothe are falthe teeth, you thupid tholithitor. Anyone could have tholen them! Anyone could have done all that biting and the nibbling of Bootleg Beth'th ear!'

I could see Spoon thinking about this. I could always tell when Spoon was a-thinking because a glazed look seizes his eye and he starts to hum quietly to himself. He couldn't deny she was right.

'You're right. Your teeth are guilty, but you are not. I'll take the teeth back to prison – you are free to go.'

Before Spoon could change his mind, we were out

of the door and on the street, slapping high-fives and chuckling merrily.

Ha! A victory for the crew of the Naughty Lass! We'd sunk 'Greasy' Spoon's battleship good and proper. Molly was free as a salmon and 'twas time to celebrate. 'Twas grand to have Moll back aboard and a home-coming party was in order. She hugged us all as she stepped over the threshold of her old home and danced a merry jig when she saw our sign:

WELCOME HOME, MOLLY MEAKINS – TOUGH AND RUTHLESS, ROUGH AND TOOTHLESS!

We'd splashed out on a magnum of grog and we were just about to plunge into a party pack of crab sticks when a loud crashing and a banging came from the hall. Spot flew from the room, a paper party hat still on his head, and opened the front door. Lola Schwartz erupted into the hall like a geyser and burst into the front room.

She surveyed the merriment and all fell silent.

'Jellied eels and ice cream, eh?' she said.

Ho had worked hard cooking up the grub for the party and offered Lola a plate of something green with

a candle in it. She ignored him and shot a furious look at Spot, who squawked and hid under my tunic. I waved a little party flag. But 'twas not me she wanted to see. Her eyes fell on Moll.

'Molly Meakins? Free at last, eh?'

Molly nodded sheepishly, but continued slurping her trifle through a straw. 'Just because your teeth are guilty,' continued Lola, 'it doesn't mean your mouth wasn't around them when the crime was committed, you know.'

Then she turned back to me. 'So, Sam Hawkins, award-winning Pirate Detective!' I smiled my most charming of smiles and nodded.

'Tomorrow, as you may know, is Friday.'

I looked towards the calendar on the wall and nodded my agreement.

'And Friday is the grand opening of the Rockness Monster Rock Festival.'

I nodded again, a little slower this time.

'And, so far, we have the stadium, we have the merchandise stalls, we have a whole load of dignitaries, but we don't have—'

'The lighthouse.' I finished off her sentence.

'Yes, I know. You see, 'tis not proving an easy case, your worshipfulness. However, I am on the trail and will soon have the lighthouse in my palm.'

I grabbed a fish stick and brandished it triumphantly

in the air.

Lola leaned closer to me.

'So, you're saying you'll have the light-house in place in the centre of the stadium ready for tomorrow's opening?'

'Well . . .'

She snatched the crab stick from my hand and popped it in her mouth.

'Good! That's all I needed to know.' And with that she strode to the door.

'Twas then she stopped and turned slowly, very slowly, back to us.

'Oh, by the way, my dear friend Harvey Clump wants you to know that the Rockness Monster Rock Festival means a lot to him. He's spent a lot of money on it and he's going to earn a lot of money from it. If the lighthouse isn't there, then he's going to send his friends to see you.'

'That'll be nice!' I said, waving my little party flag once more.

Lola smiled her most bewitching smile and took the flag from me.

She locked her eyes with mine and snapped the flag in two. I made a small squeaking sound, which I hoped the crew hadn't heard.

'And his friends will make you walk the plank . . .'

183

Pah! What manner of threat was that? I had walked many a plank and bobbed to the surface to tell the tale. She didn't frighten me.

'. . . off the top of Clump Tower!'

I made a louder squeaking sound as Lola left the room.

The silence in the room was broken only by the sound of Moll slurping her trifle.

The next morning I was a-twiddling my neckerchief and getting my brain into all sorts of nautical knots. This was the deepest, darkest mystery I'd ever come across in all my days on the blue briny. Not a crumb of a clue had proved any use and now poor old Molly had lost her teeth. I looked up at the picture of my old mum on the mantelpiece. 'Grapeshot' Betty Hawkins! Finest woman ever to have put to sea. What would she have done in my place, I wondered – probably cracked open another keg of gin and danced a hornpipe. Ho and Moll were the greatest crew I'd ever sailed with, but neither had come up with the goods and old Hawkins himself was a-lost, adrift on this huge ocean of a mystery.

I found a pickled egg in a drawer in the kitchen and chomped the end off it.

At that point I heard the televisual box cackle, and

my ears were drawn to a special announcement. I wandered into the living room and sat next to Ho, who had the remote still in his hand.

The camera was panning across the Rockness Monster Rock Festival stadium. It seemed all was a frantic flutter of activity. Scaffolding everywhere and hard-hatted men scurrying back and forth with all manner of building bits and bobs. 'Twas built upon Pointy Head Cliff and a hearty gale was blowing. A large banner flapped in the wind: 'Sponsored by Clump Enterprises!' it declared.

Behind that was the Sleepy Lagoon, a tourist spot popular for years in Washed-upon-the-Beach and this year to be the location for the main part of the opening celebrations.

The camera came to rest on the reporter, who stared through the screen at us without blinking. How do they do that?

'And so the great day dawns. A moment of history is being created here in Washed-upon-the Beach.' He swept his arm and gestured towards the looming stadium. 'The final touches are being added as we speak. But one question remains unanswered: "Where is the Pointy Head Lighthouse?" Only one person knows the answer . . .'

And at that point they flashed a picture of me on the screen. 'Twas me on the telly. I nudged Ho gleefully.

'Sam Hawkins, Pirate Detective,' the report continued. 'Of course, if old Sam fails to recover the lighthouse . . .'

He drew a pointed finger across his throat and made a garrotting sound. Ho nudged me back gleefully.

'And the grand opening ceremony will contain a very special performance. The Battle of Trafalgar will be re-created on Sleepy Lagoon by the famous Portuguese Men-of-War Synchronized Swimming Display Team. The Portuguese Men-of-War have re-created sea battles all over the world and are famous for their historical accuracy and sea shanties. But—' The reporter suddenly stopped and poked his finger in his ear. He seemed to listen very carefully to his finger, then said, 'Breaking news – we've just heard that two dolphins have broken free from the Washed-upon-the-Beach Aquarium. Scampy and Chips were loved by children of all ages . . .'

The picture fizzled out as I stabbed the button on the remote.

'What are you doing, bum-face?' Ho asked. 'It's *Tiddlywinks* on next.'

But my mind was elsewhere. The Portuguese Men-of-War! What a stroke of luck. I hadn't laid eyes on them for many a year. They used to be a cutthroat band of oyster smugglers hacking out a living in the Algarve. But in recent years they'd turned their dirty hands to more decent employment. Synchronized swimming. Ha! The perfect pursuit for a retired buccaneer. Second only to being a private detective, I thought. 'Twould be a joy to share tales of days gone by. They'd still remember me – we'd stolen many a scallop together. And maybe, just maybe, they might be able to help me with the case.

Chapter Sixteen

I sat quietly in the hold of the Naughty Lass, flicking my bottom lip and wondering how best to approach the Portuguese Men-of-War when the telephone tinkled into life. I snatched it from the cradle and held it to my shell-like.

'Sam Hawkins, award-winning Pirate Detective!' I announced. My heart turned cold as I heard the reply.

'This is the Scarlet Winkle speaking!'

Blowholes! 'Twas the very villain I sought. I needed to think quickly! I quickly thought. I ummed and ahhed. Then a flash of inspiration came. I pinched my nose between two fingers and spoke.

'I'm away solving a crime at the mo. At the tone leave your name, rank and serial number and I'll get back to you.' I then dinged the ship's bell for the tone and listened intently.

'This is the Scarlet Winkle!' spat the sinister voice

 I'd heard before. 'What a fool you are, Hawkins. I have the lighthouse – you have the clues. What more does a detective need?'

He was about to say something else when there were sounds of a struggle and another voice came on the phone. And this one was singing: 'My *lighthouse lies over the ocean, my lighthouse lies over the sea, my lighthouse lies over the ocean, oh, bring back my lighthouse to me!*'

Then there was yet another struggle and I listened intently as the first voice returned. 'I said no singing!'

And the phone went silent. I couldn't believe my ears.

I sat and pondered. 'Twas time to admit I needed help – I needed the Portuguese Men-of-War.

Sleepy Lagoon sat quietly near the Pointy Head Cliff and at the heart of the Rockness Monster Rock Festival stadium. 'Twas a fine old pond, much visited by tourists interested in its maritime history. 'Twas here that Tommy Pumper had cooled his aching feet after the Marathon Hornpipe of 1852. 'Twas here that Admiral 'Splash' Gordon had sunk the queen's flagship. ('Twas only a model, but she wasn't happy about it and had his model admiral beheaded on the spot!)

But today the lagoon was being used for another purpose. Here the rehearsals were taking place for the opening ceremony of the Rockness Monster Rock Festival. I sat on the edge of the water and watched the Battle of Trafalgar re-created before my eyes.

A Portuguese Man-of-War paddled a large pedalo, dressed like HMS *Victory*, into the centre of the lagoon. Another appeared dressed like the Spanish Armada. The costume was accurate, but the history wasn't, I thought, as I unwrapped my lunch. Another pedalo paddled into view. Written across its tiny hull was the word *Titanic*. That should go down well, I giggled into my sandwich.

The lagoon was fed by Clackitt's Canal, which ran parallel with the Great White Rail Company railway line. I gazed across and imagined how, in years gone by, the barges and trains would race madly side by side, whistles blowing and steam fluming. Ah, those were the days, I thought, pulling something black and wiggly from my sandwich, but no one gets steamed up about trains any more. I giggled again at my joke and coughed on a radish. I scooped out something else from my lunchbox and nibbled it. It tasted like it might nibble back.

Suddenly, a flare went up and a rousing naval ditty was piped through the speakers. And the battle began. Well, 'twas more like a scuffle than a battle. Every bang was a pop and every war-cry a whimper. Where once brave sailors had hacked and thrust their way to a triumphant victory, here three slightly overweight men poked each other with plastic swords. Where was the dazzling swordplay? Where were the flying sparks as iron hit iron? What about the ear-shattering reports of cannons? I'd heard louder party-poppers!

There was another small explosion and the *Titanic* started to sink. The captain saluted as he went down with his ship. Unfortunately, the lagoon was only a few centimetres deep, so he didn't go down very far. The spectacle fizzled to a finish and my lunch crunched to a stop. I packed away my treasure-chest lunch box and I applauded as the performers waded ashore.

The Portuguese Men-of-War numbered seven in total and they were now sitting on the edge of the lagoon, towelling the sweat from their brows and the muddy water from their feet.

As I drew nearer, I saw Antonio, everyone's favourite Man-of-War. In his prime he had been the hunkiest oyster smuggler at sea. Maidens swooned whenever he entered a tavern and men everywhere envied his toned body. Despite the passage of time, his muscles still rippled – even from this distance, I could

see them a-rippling. He was kneeling by a small camping stove, no doubt preparing some hearty Portuguese broth for his co-pirates.

'Hey-nonny-nonny!' I cried, like in the days of old, and slapped my thigh. It hurt a little. I was about to plunge into some Portuguese I vaguely remembered from my time at sea. Luckily I was in luck.

'What do you want?' growled Antonio in broken English, drawing himself up to his full height – which was quite a high height, I noticed. He could have been a successful window cleaner if he'd wanted, I thought. I shook the thought out of my head and introduced myself.

''Tis I, Sam Hawkins, Pirate Detective. Your old pal!'

Antonio picked up the ladle and, with his bare hands, bent it in two before my eyes.

'Never heard of you,' he said.

'Sam Hawkins, I was your number-one fan. I used to write to you every day. I once sent you a fish finger to sign!'

'Oh, *that* Sam Hawkins!'

I stepped forward so Antonio could take in the full splendour of me. Within seconds a strange smell was washing around my nostrils. Whatever they were cooking, it had a stench worse than any Ho had ever made.

Antonio turned his attention away from me and started dishing out the soup – not an easy task with a bent ladle.

'Twas at this point I felt a strange heat at my feet. I looked down to see that I had inadvertently knocked over the camping stove, which in turn had set light to the dry grass around it. I decided action was needed. I grabbed a jug that was lying on the ground and scurried over to the lagoon. I scooped up a decent dollop of dirty water and returned. Just as I was about to pour it over the fire, a hand snatched it from me.

'Just what we need!' said Antonio. 'You are a good man.' And with that he poured a small measure into the waiting mugs of all his colleagues. They made a Portuguese toast and raised their mugs.

I was just about to cry, 'No!' when they swallowed. Heigh-ho, I thought, and quietly I stamped out the fire with my foot.

Antonio grabbed me playfully by the chin. 'You are a good man. Look, I flex my pecs for you!'

And then a strange thing occurred. Just as Antonio was flexing his muscles, one of the Men-of-War, a chunky hunk to my left, suddenly twitched, his lips wiggled like two eels and his face turned an odd shade of green.

Next another fellow let out a burp as loud as gunshot and hugged his stomach. Meanwhile, to his left the tallest Man-of-War was making a strange sucking noise and fell to the ground. Slowly, all seven of the Men-of-War collapsed in a coughing, burping heap, clutching their bellies.

I twiddled my thumbs and gazed innocently about.

Antonio looked around at his men, then back at me.

'What was in that jug?' he asked, as he stopped flexing.

'Look at the time!' I said, studying my bare wrist. 'Must be off!' And with that I showed my stern and high-tailed it away from the lagoon.

As I left I heard a grisly groan from Antonio as he collapsed.

The Naughty Lass was like a desert island on my return. Not a solitary sole was about. Good job, too. They would be asking me questions like, 'Why are you sweating so much?' and 'Why are you putting a chair against the door?'

I flapped open the letter box and peered out to see if I had been pursued, but Puddle Lane was as quiet as the darkest deep. I sighed with relief and collapsed into my creaky, squeaky rocking chair, drawing a paper and a quill from my pocket. The pen is mightier than the sword, I thought, as I swished my quill through the air, but I didn't think it would hold up against the Portuguese Men-of-War. I turned my thinking to the Scarlet Winkle. I had been taunted by the very villain we were looking for and needed to think, and quickly.

The voice on the telephone reminded me of someone, someone I know well. I could feel it in my water. Could it be Long John Saliva? I knew he was caught up in the crime, but 'twas not him. We've spat and gobbed our way across the globe together. I'd recognize his voice anywhere – with or without a nut in his mouth.

Who then? Who would taunt me in such a way? Who would know all the ins and outs of the case so far?

Tinkle, tinkle.

I leapt out of my seat as the phone rang. I was as jumpy as a freshly netted haddock. My hand hovered over the receiver, but then I stopped. Should I answer it?

I pushed the quill behind my ear and a little ink dribbled down my neck. Are you a sailor or a sea-horse, I asked myself. I snatched the receiver from the cradle and held it to my shell-like.

'If this is the Scarlet Winkle, then I'm an award-winning detective!' I wiggled my Golden Albatross at the phone. 'And I'm hot on your stern.'

There was a long silence. Then a voice I recognized spoke.

'What are you talking about, Hawkins?' asked Lola Schwartz.

'Nothing, just practising my new ad campaign. "Take fright, villains of all sizes, Sam is on your tracks" or "Sam Hawkins, mystery solver" or "Sam Hawkins—"'

The Mayor interrupted me. 'Sam?'

'Yes, boss?'

'Stop talking now.'

'Yes, boss.' I clenched the phone tighter. She shouldn't talk to an old sea-dog like that, but then she is the boss.

'Now, Hawkins, do you know anything about the sudden illness that has affected the Portuguese Men-of-War?'

I paused. I was a noble seaman and I had to tell the boss the truth.

'No,' I said, biting my knuckle.

'Hmm,' replied the Mayor. 'Well, it seems that some idiot has poisoned them with lake water . . .'

'Really?' I said, but then a thought occurred. 'But what about the opening ceremony of the rock festival?'

'I know.'

'People come from miles—'

'I know.'

'The town could lose lots of money.'

'I know.'

'And maybe they'll never return.'

'Stop talking, Sam.'

'Yes, boss.'

I tangled my fingers around the phone's cord as she spoke.

'So I have had to book an alternative act. I needed someone to step in at the last minute and perform the sea-battle re-creation.'

'Who did you get?'

'The Sea Scouts!'

Oh, cod fish – the Sea Scouts.

'Excellent – the Sea Scouts!' I said, strangling the cord wire.

'By the way, Hawkins, something has happened which might interest you. Come up and see me when you've nothing on.'

I was stumped by the invitation.

'Could I just wear my hat?' I asked, but the phone had already gone dead.

Chapter Seventeen

I leapt aboard the Nippy Clipper like the eagerest of salmons and sped at a rare rate of knots towards the Washed-upon-the-Beach town hall.

What juicy morsel of information had fallen in Lola Schwartz's pretty little lap? What succulent bit of bait was she dangling before me?

I screeched to a halt before the dusty building and ran up the steps.

I slapped my sweating palm on the desk bell, but the dingling failed to turn a head. I dingled again. I looked about, hopping from foot to foot.

'Can I help you?' a man hove into view. He had a face like a well-battered plaice.

'I'm dingling!' I said, pointing at the bell.

'What can we do for you?' he replied, moving the bell out of my reach.

'I wish to see Lola Schwartz!'

The man looked at me as if I was something he'd found floating in his tea, then he picked up a book. On the front it said 'Appointments'.

'Do you have an appointment?' He took a deep breath before adding, 'Sir.'

What was wrong with this fool? Didn't he recognize my famous nautical fizzog?

'No, I am Sam Hawkins, Pirate Detective!' I triumphantly announced.

On those words, the entire room fell silent and, like a shoal of well-trained dolphins, all heads turned towards me. Ah, now they recognized me. I could tell this, as they were pointing and murmuring. But this was no time for vanity, I thought, I must solve the case.

The man looked at me and shivered. Obviously he'd never been so close to fame before. He slammed the appointment book shut.

'No appointment, sorry, goodbye!' He disappeared into the shoal of workers, all of them now focused on sharpening pencils, watering plants and whistling.

Curses and tadpoles!

I reached across the desk and dingled the bell again.

And again.

And once more for luck, but didn't get any.

Ha! This slimy trove of pen-pushers are not going

to get the better of Sam Hawkins, I thought, as I slid my quill from my pocket. I delicately leaned over the desk and nabbed the Appointments book.

I scratched the following words upon it:

Sam Hawkins to see Lola Schwartz — 4 p.m.

Then I slid it back across the desk.

I coughed to gain the little man's attention once more.

I coughed again and dingled the bell.

I coughed, dingled the bell, sneezed and shouted, 'Oops, a pelican!'

Finally, the little man reluctantly ambled over.

'Hello . . .' He sighed, and seemed to have trouble recalling me. 'Mr—'

I adjusted my neckerchief and proudly announced, 'I am Sam Hawkins, Pirate Detective, and I have an appointment with Lola Schwartz.'

'No, you don't,' he replied.

'Yes, I do.'

'No, you *don't*.'

'I think you'll find I do,' I said, tapping the Appointments book.

The man tore open the book and pointed at the page for today. And there was my appointment, as bold as a sea bass. The man looked at the book a couple of times and held it to the light.

'Nice handwriting,' he murmured. 'Looks like someone has used a quill, not standard council issue, but there we are.' He shrugged, filled in a security pass and handed it over.

'Floor 12!'

Ha! At last! Now I would find out what the lovely Lola had in store for me. Now I would know what juicy clue she had nestling in her pretty palm.

'Oh, and another thing, sir . . .' I reversed back to the desk. 'Don't forget your quill . . .'

I snatched the implement from his grasp and made for the lifts.

Gentle music breezed through Lola's office as I entered. 'Twas a CD of sea shanties played on pan pipes. Ah, 'twas music to soften the hardiest of hearts. I swayed under the bewitching spell of the tunes, my thoughts momentarily adrift. Only the toughest of sea-farers could resist the charms of such beautiful sounds.

'Can you believe this garbage?' barked Lola, ripping the CD from its moorings and scuppering a delightful rendition of 'Molly Malone'.

She hurled the CD out of the window and, in the distance, a seagull squawked.

'Just because I'm Mayor of a seaside town, everyone

thinks I love the sea!' She slumped in her chair and sipped a coffee.

'And you don't?' I asked, astounded.

'Oh, yeah, I love the sea.' she said, as I sat. 'From a distance. Say fifty or sixty kilometres. Can we talk about the case, please?'

I sat up straight and awaited what I had come for.

Lola sat up too and leaned across her desk conspiratorially.

'I gotta clue!' she said, then she giggled.

'Twas like the gleeful sound of a proud puffin after its very first swim. And with that giggle she produced a mobile phone from her filing cabinet. With a fine finger she flipped open the phone and held it towards me. I dodged slightly, not being used to these new-fangled instruments.

Inside the phone was a little screen. I wasn't sure what it was going to do next.

'Do you understand?' asked Lola.

'Not really,' I said, playing with a stapler.

She waved the phone at me.

'I've been sent a picture!' she said eagerly. 'Me!'

She stabbed the phone and a picture shimmered into a view. I squinted and leaned closer. What I saw sent a shiver down my spine, across my thigh and out of my big toe.

There, in full colour, inside Lola's little phone, was

a picture of the Scarlet Winkle. I knew it was the Scarlet Winkle, because he had the initials S.W. on his little costume – 'Scarlet Winkle'.

'Twas an odd sight – not a good photo. But it revealed more information than we had gained so far. 'Twas what we experts call a profile shot. That is to say, only one side of him was showing. His left side. And he was clad in odd attire. A little red mask covered his head. Then, across his chest, was a red jerkin on which were the letters S.W., and hanging from his little neck was a red cape. This was finished off with red tights. Red tights? And little red shoes. He looked like a tandoori lobster.

'And that, Sam Hawkins, is the Scarlet Winkle!' She snapped shut the phone and gazed at me. 'So what are you going to do?'

I scratched my grizzled chin and considered my next move.

'How did you get the photograph?'

'It's from one of our security cameras.'

'And where is this security camera situated?'

'At the entrance to the old disused railway tunnel by the canal.'

I pulled at my bottom lip and considered my next move.

'We could distribute the photo around town to see if anyone recognizes it . . . We could put it on *Police Watch* and ask if there were any witnesses . . . We could find out where he got his little red costume made . . . We could—'

Lola grabbed me by the neckerchief and almost dragged me across the desk. 'Or you could simply visit the disused tunnel and find out why he was there.'

I untangled myself from the Mayor's grip and slid back into my chair.

'That was my next suggestion.'

And with that I stood up and turned for the door.

'Sam!' The Mayor stopped me with her cry. 'Go winkle out the Winkle!'

I saluted and left.

'Penknife, string, rope, deodorant, torch, pickled egg . . .'

I was in my bedroom in the Naughty Lass, excitedly filling my bag with useful detective tools. I was doing it as quietly as possible, but I was anxious to solve this slippery case, and its conclusion was not far over the horizon. Normally, I would ask Molly and Ho to accompany me.

'Fly swat, chewing gum . . .'

But I needed to sail solo on this part of the voyage. They would be heavy cargo, weighing me down. I had to be free to switch direction like the sleekest of schooners, and besides, there might be some reward money involved.

'Mouse trap, calculator, clean socks . . .'

I zipped up the bag, took a deep breath and tiptoed to the bedroom door.

I stepped on to the landing. A plank creaked under my weight. I tensed, but no one emerged. All was silent as the deep.

I made for the stairs and padded down, with my bag slung across my shoulders.

I crept into the corridor, careful not to make any sound.

I placed my hand on the door knob, and then I heard two familiar voices.

'Can we come?'

I turned to see Molly and Ho gazing at their boss.

I placed a caring hand on Ho's shoulder. What could I say to this noble pair of heroes, these fine buccaneers who were like brothers to me?

'No!' I said, and opened the door.

'But we're detectives too, fish-face!' moaned Ho. 'We want to help solve the mystery.'

I turned again. Molly and Ho had followed me on to the driveway.

'Not this time, crew. Who knows what dangers may be out there!'

Molly crept over to me.

'Yeth, naughty people . . .' she said toothlessly. 'Evil villainth . . . Monthterth . . . Ghothtth . . . Thtrange creatureth that nibble your toeth . . . . . .'

'All of that, yes,' I said, feeling a little uneasy at the thought.

'What shall we do, then, great and wondrous boss?' asked Ho.

I spoke gently. 'I have the perfect job for you. If the telephone rings, I want you and Molly to use all your nautical know-how and answer it.'

Molly looked at Ho and Ho looked at Molly.

'Is that it?'

'Yep!' I said, and leapt over the gate and scurried off down Puddle Lane.

The sun was slipping over the horizon as I walked stealthily through the back streets of Washed-upon-the-Beach. I went past endless terraced houses, I traipsed past the Benbow Recreation Ground, I even passed a bush from which came the sound of scratching. I stopped at the scratching bush. Maybe it was a lost hedgehog or a sleepwalking squirrel. I was so busy wrestling with my imagination that I failed to see a shadowy figure leap out and lurch towards me. I clutched my bag to my chest.

'I have string in this bag and I'm not afraid to use it!' I yelled.

I squeezed my eyes tight shut, as all well-trained detectives do in emergencies.

'Sam Hawkins!' said a voice I recognized.

I opened my eyes and stared at the owner of the voice.

'It's me!'

'Twas Long John Saliva.

'My old deck-swabbing pal, you gave me the collywobbles.' I placed a hand on my heart. 'I think it's still wobbling!'

Then another thought occurred.

'Wait a blithering moment – you're my prime suspect. You stole the Pointy Head Lighthouse! Now you're trying to steal my string!'

Long John placed a hand on my shoulder.

'That's not what I was doing. I was coming to see you. I am not guilty of any crime!'

I drew my face closer to his face.

'But you attacked Billy Buddy!'

Long John squirmed uncomfortably.

'Because I knew he had the little lighthouse, which was worth money. More money than a poor musician like me could make in a lifetime. I was consumed with envy. I wanted the coins!'

We started to walk on. I was beginning to trust

207

Long John once again. But I still had one question.

'Would you tell me if you *had* stolen the light-house?'

'Of course not . . .'

'See – I have a point!'

Then a thought nudged the other thought out of the way.

'Wait a minute. How tall are you?'

We both stopped and I looked him up and down, both ways.

'Six four, in a favourable wind!'

Ha! The anchor dropped. I knew Long John was innocent. And how did I come to this conclusion? Lola's picture of the Scarlet Winkle showed a man much shorter than Long John. 'Twas proven proof he was as innocent as a herring. We started to walk on and I patted him on the back.

'I know you didn't steal it. I never doubted you. I am currently close on the fins of the vile villain who did, though.'

'Can I come too?'

''Fraid not, matey, this I must do alone!'

Long John stopped once more. I threw my bag over my shoulder and, with a jaunty salute, skipped off.

'But, Sam, out there could be monsters and ghouls and strange things that go plop in the night, creatures of uncertain origin, creatures that nibble—'

'All right, all right, you can come, but you will have to carry the bag!'

Long John ran after me and together we set off on the final league of our voyage.

Chapter Eighteen

The evening was drawing on as we approached the entrance to the disused railway tunnel. 'Twas a daunting and dark place. It gaped open like the mouth of a surprised whale. Long John Saliva and I picked our way through the overgrown railway tracks and padded towards it, hushing each other as we went.

I halted at the opening and Long John halted into me.

'My foot!' I hissed. 'Get off my foot! I need it!'

'Sorry!'

A large white, grime-riddled sign stood by the entrance to the tunnel. Its message was clear:

**By order of the Great White Rail Company –
DANGER!
Trespassers will get lost!**

So this was the last place the Scarlet Winkle had been seen. He could have found a nicer one, I thought, as I stepped in another puddle. But I had no other course to chart and ahead was my destiny. I gulped a dry gulp and took a tentative step into the gaping chasm. My footfall echoed down the tunnel. With Long John close on my stern, we entered.

'Twas a strange and eerie place. With only my torch for guidance, we padded through the puddles without a plan in mind. I chose not to think about whatever was squelching beneath our feet. Whatever it was, it was giving off the most hideous of pongs.

Long John was holding his nose as we tramped and spitting the occasional nut to amuse himself. With deadly accuracy he hit a rusty lamp, a bird's nest and me on the back of the head.

I stopped suddenly and held up my hand to silence Long John.

'I haven't said anything!' he said, removing an unlaunched peanut from his mouth.

Being a finely trained pirate, I knew something was odd. I placed my palm to my shell-like and listened.

Far, far in the distance I heard a strange sound – 'twas like the buzz of a merry bee. Clearly some sort of

shanty. Suddenly it stopped and I heard a gibbering argument. Then that too disappeared.

I beckoned Long John to follow and we plunged deeper into the tunnel.

On and on we crept.

And then we saw it. Up ahead, lit by a dim lamp, was a magnificent sight. 'Twas a fine and shiny steam engine standing majestically in the tunnel. Its perfectly polished livery was twinkling in the slight light and huffing puffs of steam were popping from its funnel. Across its grand belly were the words 'The Chuffing Shunter'. I slapped my thigh in surprise. I was so surprised I almost slapped Long John's too. This was the selfsame engine I had spied the other day, hurtling along the railway at a rapid rate of knots. Ha!

Suddenly a figure emerged from the cab, like a worker bee leaving the hive. It flittered and skittered about. I pushed Long John into the shadows and hushed him. He almost swallowed his peanut.

'I'm not saying anything, again,' he hissed.

And then the bickering stopped as suddenly as it had started. I pressed my ear to the darkness and heard the faint tip-tap of disappearing footsteps. The figure was gone, but when would he be back?

Slowly and carefully, and squelching as quietly as possible, I approached the engine. I ran my torch beam across its hull.

'Twas a beauty, no doubt about it, but what part did it play in the Scarlet Winkle's dastardly plan? Was it an escape route? Was it here to put us off the scent? I wished it would put us off the scent in the tunnel! 'Twas a proud and shiny machine – though I'm a man of the sea, I could tell a powerful trundler when I saw one. And I was looking at one right now.

'What do you suppose the Winkle's plan is?' whispered Long John, ambling up behind me.

'Knowing the Scarlet Winkle as well as I do, I would say something is slithering through the deep recesses of his brain . . .'

'So what's he up to?'

'Something deep and devious . . .'

'What?'

'I don't know! But whatever it is, you can bet your sea-bottom dollar it will include this mighty machine!'

'Twas time to dive deeper into the murky depths of this mystery. I walked slowly behind the shunter and encountered a curious carriage coupled to the rear of the engine. And it was carrying a canvas-covered load which was cylindrical in shape. And very large. And very long. 'Twas about the same length as . . . But no, it couldn't be . . . Could it?

I placed a hand on the ropes which lashed the canvas to the carriage and sneakily slipped a knot undone.

213

Slowly, very slowly, I peeled back the canvas. Long John gasped and a peanut whistled through the air, lodging itself in my nose. I sneezed and it plopped in a puddle. I looked up and Long John was pointing in disbelief.

'The Pointy Head Lighthouse!' he cried.

The evil Scarlet Winkle was trying to make off with our precious lighthouse, was he? Clearly he was planning to tow the lighthouse to another town and try to off-load it on some stupid sucker! The sneaky seagull!

'Twas at that point I heard a rustling.

I placed a silencing finger to my lips. Long John glared at me, but said nothing. I snapped off my torch

'Twas a rustling and a grunting.

'Twas a rustling and a grunting and a giggling.

Behind the large canvas-covered carriage was a smaller carriage with a red flag to mark the end of the train. It too was covered in canvas.

Long John and I moved slowly towards it. In the darkness I could make out a lump under the canvas and next to it a slightly smaller lump. I rummaged in my bag to find something to defend myself with. I pulled out a fly swatter – not ideal, I thought, flitting it in the air, but 'twould do. Long John loaded his mouth with a walnut.

Long John and I quietly counted down from three to one and then, with a mighty yelp, lurched towards the wriggling lumps.

'Caught you, you cowardly carp!' I yelled. 'You'll never steal our lighthouse!'

Long John whipped off the canvas and uncovered the loathsome load.

I snapped on my torch and pointed it.

'Hello, boss!' said Molly and Ho.

What? Double what? I polished my torch and pointed it again. I squinted. I prodded them with my fly swatter. But there was no doubt about it – 'twas them! And Spot was behind them, waving his wing.

'My timbers have never been so shivered! You mucky buccaneers! What are you doing here?'

Ho slid from his hidey-hole.

'Thought you might need a little help, bothth!' Molly followed and landed in a puddle, emptying it of its contents, which covered me instead.

I glared at her gummy face.

'But if you don't want uth we can alwayth . . .' she said, and started to remount the little carriage.

Spot made a huffing noise.

'All right, all right, you can help me with the case. We're nearly home and dry anyway. All we have to do is wait for the crafty criminal to return and we'll ensnare him. The Scarlet Winkle'll be caught like a sprat up a drainpipe!'

Suddenly, Long John placed a finger to my lips and said quietly, 'Hush!'

'Get your dirty finger off my dirty lips!' I shouted. 'I'm in charge – I do the hushing!' I looked about at my silent crew. 'Sshh!' I said quietly.

Long John pointed up ahead. 'Twas a sound. The sound of footsteps. The footsteps of the villain were returning and bringing the villain with them. Was this the evil Scarlet Winkle who'd been leading us a merry dance for so long? Were we on the brink of netting the vilest pilchard ever to plumb the depths of the underworld? We all looked at each other and, like one well-oiled crime-fighting unit, we slipped aboard the little carriage and pulled the canvas over us.

We waited.

Inside was dark and dank and smelt slightly of fish.

Molly spoke very quietly. 'Why are we hiding, bothth? Can't I jutht grab him and thtick hith head in the funnel?'

'No, my eager trout,' I whispered. 'I have a snorkellingly good plan. If we stay hidden in this carriage, we'll get towed behind the lighthouse by the Chuffing Shunter and we'll end up wherever the Pointy Head Lighthouse is being taken!'

'So?' said Ho, sniffing the air, then holding his nose.

'So, then we leap out and net both the Scarlet Winkle and whoever is buying the lighthouse in one fell swoop!'

'Fell swoop!' echoed Spot.

With that I heard the hurling and shovelling of coal into the belly of the beast. The engine roared its hungry thanks by way of a shrill hooter. The sound echoed down the tunnel. I pressed my ear to the side of the carriage and heard dark

mutterings and arguings as the engine started. Were there two of them? No, surely my seagull eye had spotted only one.

I felt Ho tugging at my sleeve.

'Not now, Ho, my ears are doing some detecting!'

The engine was building up steam. I could hear the gush bellowing from its spout.

'Sam!' hissed Ho.

'What?'

Ho pointed a finger at the other carriage. I was confused.

'Well, what is it?'

'*This* carriage isn't attached to *that* one!'

I grabbed his still-pointing finger and spied along it to the direction it was pointing. Cod fish!

Barnacles! There, curled up like a retired eel on the carriage deck, was a rope. I had to think quickly. What should I do? I stuck my head in my bag. What piratical tool had I brought along for just this sort of emergency?

'Nothing!' I said, as I emerged.

Then a thought plopped into my watery brain and within seconds I was turfing Ho out of the carriage with these directions: 'Get aboard the other carriage, hurl me that rope and I shall attach it! Ha, the Winkle won't escape our clutches!'

Ho jumped lightly down from our carriage and on to the squelching ground.

'I've trodden in something!'

'Never mind that! Hurry up and jump aboard!'

I peered into the darkness and could just make out Ho's little body scuttling up the side and on to the carriage carrying the lighthouse.

Seconds were slipping down the plughole and the engine was beginning to roar into life. The puffing steam was getting louder and the mighty engine was raring to be unleashed on to the tracks.

Spot and Molly swayed anxiously by my side.

And then there was a noise.

FUFF!

And then another.

FUFF!

And the engine lurched forward. Curses and cuttle-fish! Where was that cabin boy?

FUFF! FUFF! FUFF!!!

The carriage lurched forward again, placing a greater length between us and the lighthouse. I bit my nails. Molly placed a comforting hand on my shoulders. I almost bit her nails too.

Suddenly Ho's little face appeared out from under the canvas, and clutched in his hand was the rope.

'Throw it!' I hissed.

Ho hurled. But 'twas a pathetic effort and the rope landed in a heap on the ground. Ho coiled it back hastily and stood with it dangling from his hand.

'Twirl it around your head and then throw it!' I hissed.

'I know how to do it! I *am* a pirate!'

Ho twirled it around his head and threw. Once more it hit the ground beyond our grasp.

Suddenly the Chuffing Shunter shuddered and Ho was nearly knocked off his feet. He steadied himself and then he plunged his hand into his back pocket. What devious thoughts were eddying through his little brain, I wondered. But my little pal wasn't going to let me down. He was waving his catapult in the air triumphantly. Brilliant thinking, I thought, wishing I'd thought of it. Ho tied the end of the rope into a chunky knot and placed it carefully into the catapult.

Then, with a loud twong, he released it and we watched as it flew through the air. 'Twas like one of those slow-motion sequences in films where they do things slower to make it more exciting.

The rope landed on the carriage. I leapt on it like a hungry seaman netting his only catch of the day.

'Tie it to something!' hissed Ho.

'I know, I know!' I hissed back. 'I *am* a pirate!'

I looked about for a safe mooring. Below my feet was a rusty ring screwed to the planking. That'll make a secure holding point, I thought, as I tied the rope to it with a finely executed Trawlerman's Hitch. Once more the Chuffing Shunter lurched forward, but this time we would be following on behind!

I giggled and sat back to enjoy the journey.

'What did you tie it with?' asked Molly, sitting next to me.

'Trawlerman's Hitch!' I said proudly. 'Finest knot to be tied at sea.'

'The Trawlerman's Hitch? That'th a thlip knot, ithn't it?'

'A slip knot?' I queried.

'Yeth – a knot that can eathily thlide undone!'

'Yes, the trawlermen of years gone by would tie up their nets of oysters or clams, and when it was time to plop them into the crate, they'd pull the slip and off it would slide.'

'Jutht like that!' said Molly, pointing towards the slowly untying knot.

'Arghhhh!'

Molly, Long John and I leapt to our feet. Spot leapt to his claws. We all jumped at the rope, but it flopped overboard and we missed it by the skin of our fingers.

'Why didn't you tell me it was a slip knot?' I roared at Molly.

'Because you already told *me* it wath a thlip knot!' she roared back.

Curses and cuttlefish!

We stood pathetically at the end of the little carriage and gazed after the Chuffing Shunter as it chugged away in the darkness, towing behind it the Pointy Head Lighthouse. The little rope trailed behind.

On the stern of the carriage was a bewildered and flustered Ho, the rope dangling from his hand. He looked like someone who'd just lost a conker match.

But this was no time for idle thoughts, I thought, this was a time to take action.

We stood silently in the darkness and wondered what action to take.

Chapter Nineteen

What a knotty spot to be in! Chugging away before our bewildered eyes was the Chuffing Shunter, pulling the Pointy Head Lighthouse. Aboard it were the Scarlet Winkle and my cabin boy, Ho. I hurled my hat to the ground and spat out a list of curses and rude words.

'Pish and tush!' I bellowed. 'Can this get any worse?'

Molly picked up my hat, flicked off a little bit of fluff and placed it back on my head.

'It's nearly time for the opening ceremony, boss!'

I couldn't believe this! Scuppered at the final fathom! 'Twas a grimy corner we'd got ourselves into and a smelly one to boot. Spot leapt on to my shoulder and looked at me expectantly.

Long John hauled up and said, 'What shall we do now?'

'Twas a good question and I wished I had a good answer. What could I say? What crumb of hope could I offer them? I was about to speak.

'I know what we can do!' said Molly, her face an explosion of excitement. She was almost dribbling with delight. 'Follow me!'

And so saying, she beckoned towards myself and Long John and led us away. Spot flapped on behind. We crawled from the carriage and she led us along the tunnel.

Outside, evening time was covering Washed-upon-the-Beach with a snug blanket of darkness. Throughout the town little lights were coming on and above us the twinkling stars did their finest twinkling.

Molly halted and sniffed the air. What a proud sight she was – standing there silhouetted against the moonlight. If only she could spout water from her mouth, she'd look like a performing whale. She sniffed the air again.

'What cunning scheme is coursing through your nautical noggin?' I asked quietly as Spot landed on my shoulder.

She licked her thumb and held it in the air. 'Twas

an old navigational trick to discover the direction of the wind.

'Hmm, bit of trifle on my thumb!' she said brightly, 'Lovely!'

And with that we were off again. Across the cliffs via a winding old path used years ago by lobster thieves. 'Twas a sharp drop down the side but, being a brave sailor, I managed to hide my head under Molly's tunic.

Eventually we arrived safe and sound. Before us was the splendid Rockness Monster Rock Festival. The stadium was ablaze with the shiniest of bright lights. 'Twas like someone had borrowed the sun for the night. Crowds had gathered from the four corners of the town and some from corners far beyond it. All were waiting for the unveiling of the Pointy Head Lighthouse to mark the opening of the Rockness Monster Rock Festival. Fortunately, they didn't know it wasn't there. Unfortunately, I did.

We plunged into the crowd, excusing ourselves as we elbowed our way through. I saw Lola Schwartz standing on the podium, checking all was in order. Behind her was a huge red curtain. If she hadn't already looked behind it, she might at any moment. She seemed anxious. She kept peering into the crowd, like a watchman trying to spot land. Then she saw me. I waved with as much jollity as I could muster.

 224

'How long before the unveiling?' asked Long John from behind and, as if in answer to his question, Lola's voice echoed round the stadium.

'Ten minutes to the grand opening, ladies and gentlemen, ten minutes!'

She was addressing a huge crowd, but she was looking directly at me. I suddenly felt like a crab in a tank in a fish restaurant, I've no idea why.

Before the podium was the Sleepy Lagoon. The mild wind was tickling its surface and the moonlight was winking reflections at the crowd. All around the lagoon was a throng of security guards, each one wearing dark glasses and looking for trouble. Molly elbowed her way towards them; they'd found it. Squeezing her chunky bulk through the crowd, she suddenly stopped. Long John, Spot and I hauled up behind her.

She was pointing at the lagoon.

'Look!'

I looked, but all I could see were the grotty Sea Scouts, re-enacting the Battle of Trafalgar in pedalos.

'And what use is that, you dopey mermaid?'

Molly was once more elbowing her way towards the lagoon, leaving my unanswered question hanging in the air. We elbowed after her. I kept apologizing as I went, and almost lost my hat in the crowd.

Molly was on to something. She had obviously caught the scent of an idea for solving this mystery.

Pity I'd not got a whiff of it myself, but in dire times we must all pull together. And besides, it might make me famous again. I felt a small hand pulling at my sleeve. I was tugged from my thoughts by a small girl clutching an ice cream with a bright smiling face. The girl, that is, not the ice cream.

'I've seen you before!' she said merrily.

I smiled charmingly and noticed her ice cream melting slightly.

'Television!' she suddenly said, clicking the fingers on her spare hand.

I tried to be modest – it wasn't easy.

She slurped some raspberry ripple and said, 'It's still not working properly. Can you come and fix it again?'

Curses, the bratty sprat thought I was a TV repair man. Pah! I started elbowing away, narrowly missing the girl but squashing her ice cream. Ha!

At the lagoon, Molly casually slunk past two security guards and dipped a toe in to gauge the depths. The water came up to her knees. She climbed in with a couple of sploshes and ploughed on.

In the centre of the lake the poshest pedalo was resplendently dressed like HMS *Victory*. On board was a spotty Sea Scout. On closer inspection, I realized it was Bobby Buoy, the very fellow who fell into my sidecar all those days ago. He was dressed as Admiral Nelson with an eyepatch on one eye and an arm behind his back. He was holding a telescope to his patched eye.

'I see no ships!' he announced, and his microno-phoned voice echoed around the stadium. Of course he can't, I thought, he should move his eyepatch for a better view!

Molly stumbled towards him, like a mythical sea monster emerg-ing from the depths.

'What the flippin' 'eck's that?' Bobby's voice squealed around the stadium.

Spot was clawing at my shoulder with surprise. Neither of us was sure what she was up to. Long John stood by my side, nibbling a peanut.

'She's a fine lass!' he commented between chomps.

Molly snatched the side of the pedalo and waggled it. Admiral Lord Nelson suddenly grew two arms as he fell overboard. He disappeared with a scream and a gurgle. She wrapped her mighty arms round the boat's hull, dragged it to the side of the lake and, with one swift lurch, grounded it.

'Quick – save the liddle boy!'

'Twas the voice of Antonio, Portuguese Man-of-War. His merry men began stripping and donning little rubber caps. The crowd about them clapped wildly as their heroes plunged into the shallows of the lagoon. They sploshed towards the gurgling and splashing with style gained from years of showing off. I could have done it just as well myself. I turned my attention to the dripping pedalo before me.

'But what use is this, Moll?'

She was about to answer, but stopped. She wet her thumb and rubbed her ear. 'Twas an old sailor's trick for hearing things better. She put her thumb back in her mouth.

'Toothpaste!' she said.

And then, far in the distance, we heard the wail of a familiar hooter. 'Twas the hooter of the Chuffing Shunter and it was coming closer!

The panting Molly hoisted the pedalo above her head and suddenly bellowed, 'Get out of the way!' with a splat of gummy dribble.

The crowd parted like a shoal of fish.

With the pedalo held triumphantly aloft, the mighty Molly made off. Spot and I followed on behind. Long John swallowed a peanut, said, 'She really is a fine lass!' and followed on behind us.

On the crest of the hill was the railway line. I clutched my hat and my parrot, and gazed up the track in disbelief. There she blew! The mighty Chuffing Shunter! 'Twas hurtling down the track at break-neck speed, followed by the

Pointy Head Lighthouse. 'Twould pass by us at any second.

'To the canal!' shouted Molly.

Huffing and puffing, we arrived at Clackitt's Canal, and Molly tossed the pedalo into the water.

'There!' she announced, clapping her hands gleefully.

Long John looked at me.

I looked at Long John.

Spot looked at us both and shook his head.

None of us knew what was coursing through her brain.

'Follow the train in that!' she announced, pointing at the little boat bobbing in the water.

I sighed a sigh deeper than the deepest ocean.

'But we'll never catch—'

My words were drowned out by the bellowing whistle of the Chuffing Shunter as it screeched past, steam pumping from its funnel.

And as it passed I peered into the cab. 'Twas but a fleeting peer – more of a glimpse, perhaps. The shiny cab was enveloped in sooty steam. My well-trained nautical eye could just make out the knobs and wheels of the controls, but who was controlling them?

The cloggy smog parted for the tiniest of seconds, but this was enough time for old seagull-eyed Hawkins to spot the occupant. 'Twas an occupant dressed in a

little red cape with a little red mask. He had an S.W.
embroidered on his suit.

Ha! 'Twas the Scarlet Winkle. Ha and double ha!

I almost went for a triple ha!
when something strange
occurred. As the naughty
Winkle turned to collect
some coal he disappeared.
Completely vanished.
And what was stranger still,
Billy Buddy appeared in his
place. What weirdness was this? What bizarre goings-
on were going on? As I pondered this, the little carriage behind the lighthouse trundled before our eyes.
Ho gave a weak wave as he passed by.

'Twas at this point in my tale of maritime madness
the tide turned. 'Twas a moment I shall remember for
the rest of my nautical days. As I pondered my plight,
I looked down at the canal, and staring back at me
were two sleek dolphins. Dolphins? I rubbed my eyes.

'It's Scampy and Chips from the aquarium,' said
Molly and Long John together. They turned and
looked at each other. 'Ahhh!'

The dolphins poked their heads from out of the
water and winked at me. I think they winked at me.

'Grab this!' I shouted, pulling a washing line from
my bag. I had packed the bag in such a hurry, it still

had some washing on it. Long John and Molly looked at the line in surprise.

'What thall I do?' asked Molly, holding up the line, from which dangled socks and T-shirts and the like.

'Take down your knickers!'

Molly looked bewildered.

'From the line, I mean, and tie two loops at one end!'

Being well-trained nautical fellows, Molly and Long John completed the task in seconds.

'Now tie the other end to the pedalo!' I commanded.

'Twas like being at the helm of the old *Scuttle Butt* once more and the thought almost brought a tear to my salty eye.

My plucky crew members did as they were bid.

'Now throw the loops into the water!'

And as Molly and Long John followed my orders, the two dolphins poked their snouts through the loops and attached themselves firmly to the washing line. The pedalo leapt forward.

I turned, saluted my trusty crew, leapt aboard and cried, 'I've got a train to catch!'

I was off!

Long John placed an arm across Molly's shoulder as I lurched after the dolphins. Spot looked up at the stars.

The wind was in my hair, the water was spraying my face like in days of old and there up ahead was my final destiny – the Chuffing Shunter.

Chapter Twenty

'There she blows!' I cried.

Once more I was clutching the tiller of a great adventure, once more I was helming my way through the high seas – well, at least the low canals. If only the dolphin could swim a little faster.

'Come on, my proud beauties!' I bellowed. 'There'll be a banquet for you tonight!'

I cracked the washing line and the dolphins renewed their efforts. The countryside sped by at a rapid rate of knots. Despite the encroaching twilight I could make out a tree, a bush, a startled rabbit – I sped past them all. I held on to my hat with one hand and my destiny with the other. On and on we rushed. Within the batting of a duck's eye, we were side by side with the Chuffing Shunter.

As we drew level, I peered into the cabin. A confuddling sight met my eyes. First 'twas the Scarlet

Winkle, then 'twas Billy Buddy, then 'twas the Scarlet Winkle and then 'twas Billy Buddy again. The dolphins wiggled in their course to avoid some driftwood and my gaze was torn from the cab. I shook the spray from my eyes, looked back and saw exactly the same sight. Suddenly, with an almighty splash, the whole mind-boggling mystery fell into place. I clicked my fingers.

'Of course!' I yelled, almost losing control of the pedalo. One half of his body was dressed as Billy Buddy, the other half was dressed as the Scarlet Winkle.

Suddenly, his face appeared at the window of the cab, but which face was it? I now knew he had two!

'*Help me! Help me!*' cried Billy Buddy. '*I'm being kidnapped by the Scarlet Winkle!*'

That was the lighthouse keeper speaking. He then presented me with his other half.

'Quiet, you brat! I, the Scarlet Winkle, will win the day. I have Billy Buddy and I have the Pointy Head Lighthouse!'

He turned again.

'*Save me, Sam. Save me!*'

Suddenly, the Scarlet Winkle grabbed Billy Buddy by his ear and wrestled him away from the cabin window. He then rummaged in his pocket and produced something which he waggled in the air. I peered

234

through the splashing spray and realized the fiend was waving Molly's spare pair of false teeth at me. I recognized the chewing gum stuck to the palate. So it was *he* who had stolen them on that naughty night – not Long John Saliva.

He hurled the teeth at me and I just managed to grab them before they plopped into the canal.

'Is that the worst you can do?' I bellowed, clacking the dentures with one hand.

'No!' cried the Scarlet Winkle, and he started throwing hot coals at me.

I dodged each lump like a slaloming salmon.

As quickly as it had started, the tidal wave of lumps stopped. He'd run out of coal.

'Hah!' I yelled, cracking my washing line triumphantly. But what could I hurl in response? All I had was Molly's false choppers. So I shrugged and threw them. But my aim was not true.

'Curses and cuttlefish!' I cried as the chompers bounced off the side of the carriage with a loud boing and fell on the track.

Suddenly there was a sound like a thousand pieces of chalk being dragged across a thousand blackboards. There was an eruption of steam like the mightiest of geysers and there was a squealing like a thousand terrified penguins. The false choppers had wedged themselves in the front wheel of the Chuffing Shunter. The mighty trundler couldn't trundle over Molly's teeth – they were made of tough stuff. The train ground to a halt. I looked into the cab to see a frantic Scarlet Winkle running sweating hands over the controls and switches. As soon as he had changed their position, Billy Buddy craftily switched them back again. He was going nowhere and he knew it. The chase was nearly over. Or so I thought.

As the Chuffing Shunter sat panting and puffing, another sound was heard – this time from the carriage carrying the Pointy Head Lighthouse. 'Twas a cracking, straining sound. I slowed my dolphins and turned to look. The Chuffing Shunter had stopped so suddenly, it had caused the lighthouse to shift its position in the carriage and now all its weight was pressing against the canvas and securing ropes. Suddenly there was a loud twong, followed by a short twang, another twong and a couple of twings. One by one, each rope was breaking under the pressure of its load.

Twong, twang, twong, twing! 'Twas like someone clipping the strings on a cello.

The lighthouse was going to slide from its moorings and there was nothing I could do about it! I bobbed about on my pedalo and tried to work out its destination. I looked down at the base of the hill and there below was the Rockness Monster Rock Festival.

Seconds were ticking away. I heard Lola's echoing voice.

'So let's count down . . . 10!'

The Pointy Head Lighthouse slipped neatly from under the canvas like a burial at sea and started to slide along the tracks and down the hill.

And slide and slide. It gently pushed aside bushes and rocks as it went.

'My lighthouse!' yelled the Scarlet Winkle.

'*Our lighthouse!*' corrected Billy Buddy.

'9!'

Well, that was that, then. I dismounted my pedalo and patted my dolphins.

'8!'

Another failed case – all because Ho couldn't throw a rope . . . Ho! I thought.

'Ho?' I yelled.

I gazed down at the departing lighthouse and a tiny Oriental face appeared through a window and waved weakly. I watched helplessly as my confused cabin boy clung to whatever he could find inside.

'7!'

'Pull 'em harder!' shouted a voice by the shunter.

'Twas the Scarlet Winkle, frantically trying to dislodge the teeth from the path of his train. I stumbled over to him.

'Not so fast, you slippery eel!' I cried, and grabbed his arm.

'*Not me – him!*' said Billy Buddy.

'I'm sorry,' I said, and grabbed the other arm.

'6!'

Then there was a sound that grabbed the attention of all three of us. 'Twas the proud siren of an approaching liner.

'What's all that about?' I asked, as I gazed into the dimming evening light to make out a ship.

'It's SS *Starfish*!'

'5!' echoed Lola's voice.

'*Each year we do a shadow puppet of the Rockness Monster into the light beaming from our lighthouse and it makes a silhouette on the side of the Starfish. And all those people down there are expecting it!*'

I gazed down and saw the lighthouse sliding closer to the stadium.

'4!'

'No one knows how to do shadow puppets any more!' sneered the Scarlet Winkle, struggling against my grasp.

The SS *Starfish* came into view in the twilight of the evening and the crowd cheered its arrival.

'3!'

'Twas no use. I dropped on to my knees and watched as the disaster unfolded. The lighthouse was now careering directly towards the stadium. I was helpless to help. So I did the only thing any self-respecting pirate would do. I put my fingers in my ears and closed my eyes.

'2!'

Well, it's been a short but fun career as a pirate detective, I thought. But I'd reached the end of the line.

'1!'

Maybe I'll take up a gentler profession next – like crocodile wrestling.

'Zero!'

There was a swish of the curtain followed by a long, long silence.

And the silence was followed by a loud gasp.

I slowly uncovered my face. There, standing proud and erect on the podium, was the Pointy Head Lighthouse! I rubbed my eyes.

A huge cheer went up and no one noticed the lighthouse juddering ever so slightly to a standstill.

Now, I thought, should I take the Scarlet Winkle into custody or should I go and see if there's a reward for saving the lighthouse?

'Tis a difficult decision to make, I thought, as I stumbled down the hill towards the stadium, kicking rocks and bushes and shrubs as I went.

Spot swooped from above and started pecking at my ear. He was trying to tell me something. I was trying to ignore him.

'Stadium! . . . Reward!' I panted as I leapt over a hedge.

Lola was making another announcement as I stumbled and fumbled in to the stadium. I elbowed my way through the chattering, excited crowd and finally arrived at the Pointy Head Lighthouse. Spot was still pecking my ear, but I wafted him away.

I clambered on to the podium as Lola said, 'Ladies and gentlemen, the SS *Starfish* and the moment we have all been waiting for is almost here! Harvey – over to you!'

The crowd looked from the Pointy Head Lighthouse to the gleaming SS *Starfish*. Standing on the prow, almost as shiny as his ship, was Harvey Clump. In his suntanned hand was a micronophone and his words vibrated around the stadium.

'Thanks, Lola! This is a great year for Clump Enterprises and we are proud to be sponsoring the Rockness Monster Rock Festival! So without further ado we present the Rockness Monster!'

The crowd hushed in expectation.

So did I.

Nothing happened.

The fake smile almost fell from Harvey's face as he repeated, 'The Rockness Monster!'

The audience waited some more.

So did I.

Then, from inside the lighthouse, I heard a little Chinese voice.

'I can't find the socket!'

I hissed a few instructions through the letter box. Suddenly the shiniest of lights burst from the top of the Pointy Head Lighthouse. The crowd cheered wildly.

'Now do the shadow puppet!' I hissed at Ho.

And then on the gleaming side of the mighty liner, appeared the finest shadow puppet Ho's fingers could make – it was a bunny rabbit.

A confused mumble ran around the crowd, but it quickly turned into a huge cheer and wild applause.

The Sea Scout band struck up a jaunty sea shanty as I mopped my brow.

'Twas a triumph. I showed two thumbs to Lola Schwartz, who returned a quizzical shrug.

Spot leapt on to my shoulder as a battered Ho emerged from the lighthouse. I greeted them both heartily. Spot tugged at my ear and pointed towards the crowd with his wing. Pushing their way through were Long John and Molly. Clasped in their grip was

the Scarlet Winkle!

I jumped down from the podium.

'Well done, crew!' I cried, taking the Scarlet Winkle from Molly and Long John. 'I was just coming back for you!'

Officers Stump and Stibbins emerged from the crowd.

'This is the Scarlet Winkle,' I told them proudly, 'the vile villain who stole the Pointy Head Lighthouse. Take him away!'

Officer Stump produced a set of handcuffs and clicked them on the Winkle's wrist.

'How many times do I have to say it! I'm innocent – he's the guilty one!' Billy pleaded, pointing at himself.

Stump and Stibbins were confused.

Molly whispered an explanation which made them look even more con-fused. Long John solved the problem. He reached into his pocket and produced the false teeth stolen by the wicked 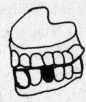 Winkle. He lovingly slipped them into Molly's mouth with a plop and gazed into her eyes. She whispered her explanation once again and the police officers finally understood.

'Very well!' announced Stibbins, with a wink. 'We will need a witness. Someone who saw the Scarlet Winkle commit all his crimes!'

'Ha! The Scarlet Winkle always works alone! No one saw me!' cackled the Winkle.

'*I did!*' snapped Billy.

'Very well,' said Stibbins. 'You'd better come along too!'

And with that Billy Buddy and the Scarlet Winkle were bundled away through the crowd.

I dusted off my hat and patted my crew once more.

''Twas a hard and tough voyage, me hearties, but once more we have found ourselves back in safe harbour.'

I was about to suggest a swift grog at the Black Spot Tavern, when someone tapped me on the shoulder. I turned to see an unfamiliar face. 'Twas a skinny man in a uniform, and a badge on his jacket read 'Washed-upon-the-Beach Aquarium'.

'Has anyone here seen my dolphins?' he asked.

I had to think quickly. I pointed up at Harvey Clump.

'Go and ask him!' I suggested.

The man looked up at the ship and when he turned back we were gone!

And so Sam Hawkins, Pirate Detective, had bravely steered his way once again through the murky waters of crime with the help of his trusty crew. I sat in my squeaky, creaky rocking chair and mused over the events of the past week.

As I pumped a nautical ditty from my squeeze-box, I slowly considered the report I was due to submit to Lola Schwartz. It would describe in precise detail what had happened. I placed my squeeze-box to one side and took up my quill.

Of course, Billy Buddy was the criminal from the beginning. Well, at least, half of him was. He was a criminal mastermind with two minds! My finely honed detecting sense had sniffed him out from the start. All I needed was a few tell-tale clues to net him. I had realized from the beginning that Billy Buddy had two distinct personalities – one a kind and caring old light-house keeper and the other a mad, crazed naughty-deed-doer called the Scarlet Winkle. And what better way for an ill-paid worker to earn extra money than a well-planned kidnapping. Fortunately, the kidnapping *wasn't* very well planned. He'd stumbled at the first lobster pot. No one would pay his ransom. Ha! So it seems that he was planning to steal the Pointy Head Lighthouse and see if he could get a good price elsewhere.

Now, you're probably wondering about Molly's teeth (a lot of people do). Well, Billy Buddy – or should I say the Scarlet Winkle? – was to blame for their sloppy snatching too. In an attempt to put us off the scent, he had sneaked into Molly's bedroom – something only a very brave or very foolish cod fish would do – and snaffled her spare pair of munchers. Then, after penning his dastardly ransom note, he broke into other folks' houses and created mayhem by leaving incriminating tooth marks in whatever he could sink her teeth into. He knew someone would measure Molly's gnashers against the tooth marks and find her guilty. That would prove enough to divert me from tracking down the lighthouse. But what the gutless guppy had forgotten was, because they were false teeth, all Molly had to do was prove they were removable. Which she did.

But what of Long John Saliva? He had overheard the price of the coins that made up the little lighthouse and was determined to nick them for himself. He failed, of course, but at heart he was a good and honest pirate and, with his band, the Spittoons, he had played a well-received set at the Rockness Monster Rock Festival. And I think he might be taking a shine to our Molly. So it looked as if he was turning his back on a life of crime for good.

Ho, Molly and Spot proved themselves, once again, the best crew members to take on a tempestuous voyage. 'Twas time I gave them their reward. But what? We had received no payment for solving this slippery case, so how could I pay them?  Then a thought plopped into my brain. Of course, the little lighthouse! The coins! Billy Buddy had promised me a handsome fee for solving the case and the handsome fee was downstairs in my ugly safe. I stabbed my quill back into its pot and galloped downstairs.

The Naughty Lass safe was stowed safely behind the settee and I knelt before it. Nervously, I slipped the key from around my neck and inserted it into the lock. I clicked open the door and there, standing proudly in the darkness, was the little lighthouse. I placed my hands over it and drew it towards me.

'Gold!' I whispered under my breath, and looked about. Then, with all my strength, I cracked it on the floor and the shining golden coins scattered about. 'Treasure!' I almost gurgled with delight. 'Treasure! My treasure!'

'Our treasure!' said three voices behind me, followed by a squawk.

I turned, and standing over me were Long John, Molly and Ho. Fluttering above was Spot.

'Yes, our treasure!' I repeated, staring at the glittering prize in my hands. Heigh-ho, I thought, as I began to distribute the crew's earnings.

All three were well-experienced pirates and had been slipped counterfeit dosh before, and so all three bit into their coins to test their authenticity.

'Imagine,' I said, 'what we could buy with this gold. Clothes, cars, maybe a new galleon . . .'

'Chocolate!' said Ho.

'Yes, I suppose you could buy some chocolate if you wanted to,' I continued.

'No,' said Ho, wiping something brown and sticky from his lips. 'These coins are made from chocolate!'

I couldn't believe my eyes or my ears. I rubbed all four. Then I grabbed a couple of coins from Molly. They almost melted in my sweaty palm.

'Cuttlefish, barnacles and blowholes!' I screamed.

Ho shrugged and slipped off into the kitchen. Long John and Molly sighed and turned away, hand in hand,

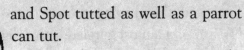

and Spot tutted as well as a parrot can tut.

I dropped to my knees, squashing the remaining chocolate coins.

'Diddled at the final fathom!' I hissed, cursing the name of Bootleg Bess, who'd let me think they were worth £1,750,000.

Suddenly, I heard an explosion from the kitchen.

I stood up and wiped chocolate from my knees.

'Ah!' I thought. 'Dinner!'

Sam Hawkins: Pirate Detective
The Case of the Cut-glass Cutlass

By Ian Billings

**Is he a pirate? Is he a detective? No!
He's the incredible, the one and only,
Sam Hawkins, Pirate Detective!**

Legendary Sam Hawkins and his trusty crew used to be the wickedest pirates on the high seas. But now they're landlubbers in Washed-upon-the-Beach, ready to right wrongs wherever they may be found (and even where they aren't).

Sam's first case is a rum one – to find the priceless Cut-glass Cutlass. But the trail leads to a treasure trove of confuddling clues: some mysteriously tiny footprints, a harmonica-playing octopus, and a distinctly pongy pile of red herrings . . .